Keeper of Secrets

Keeper of Secrets

Sarah J. Dodd

Firefly

First published in 2021
by Firefly Press
25 Gabalfa Road, Llandaff North, Cardiff, CF14 2JJ
www.fireflypress.co.uk

A CIP catalogue record of this book is available from the British Library.

1 3 5 7 9 8 6 4 2

ISBN 9781913102456
ebook ISBN 9781913102463

*This book has been published with the support of
the Books Council Wales.*

Chapter heading illustrations by Becka Moor
Typeset by Elaine Sharples

Printed and bound by CPI Group (UK) Ltd,
Croydon, Surrey, CRO 4YY

For the lonely reader: you are not alone.

1

Click!

A light came on, waking Emily with a start. A faint glow shone through the thin curtains. At first, she couldn't remember where she was. Her blanket was draped over her as usual. Everything *seemed* all right, but she felt higher than normal, as though she'd fallen asleep in a tree.

Bit by bit, last night's memories came back. The journey through the forest to Badger Cottage. Arriving late because she'd been sick in the car. The tiniest house she'd ever seen, attached to a much bigger one, like a cub clinging to its mother. A small, shabby living room with a fireplace full of cold, dead sticks. The wooden staircase with gaps between the treads, waiting to swallow her feet.

And now here she was in this bed, high up on top of a giant wooden box with a ladder at the end. The box had sliding doors so you could store things in there. A good place to hide.

A good place for anything to hide.

Her breathing sped up and she pulled the blanket over her head – the fleecy one with black-and-white patches like a giant, snuggly panda that Mum had bought for her when she'd had chickenpox. It needed a wash, really, but she liked its musty smell. It was comforting, even though she had a sneaky feeling that eleven-year-old girls should have grown out of that kind of thing.

But what was that *light*? It hadn't been on when she went to sleep. She lay still on the lumpy mattress, chewing the skin beside her fingernail. Should she stay under the covers, or should she look? She could shout for Dad, of course, but he was so grumpy if he was disturbed at night.

Peeling back the panda blanket, she sat up. She reached out to touch the curtain and hesitated. The light must be the one in the porch. It came on whenever anyone came to the front door – she remembered that from last night, when Dad had been fumbling with the key. But who would come to their door in the middle of the night? No one knew them in this village except… *Oh!* Perhaps it was Nana Godwin, come early to surprise them!

Nana Godwin. When she hugged Emily, it felt like Mum's arms in a different body; when she spoke, it was Mum's tenderness in a different voice. Tears pricked Emily's eyes. Everything would be all right if Nana were here.

Well, not all right, exactly. But even all wrong was better when Nana Godwin was around.

Emily flung back the curtain.

And froze.

Outside, padding along the lane in front of the cottage, was a beast. It was the size of a massive dog, but its face was the wrong shape – more catlike, only it had weird tufts on its ears and a stump of a tail. Its golden fur was spotted, some of the spots stretching out into black streaks. A rabbit swung from its mouth. Limp.

Dead.

The beast stopped and looked up. It must have seen her.

With a frightened squeak, Emily let the curtain fall back and pressed herself against the wall.

What if it came into the garden? What if it managed to get *in the house*? She imagined it padding through the living room and up the staircase, silent and stealthy on those massive paws. On the landing and outside her door, and … *what was that noise?*

A wailing groan, like an animal in pain. It sounded nearby. It seemed to be coming from the wall between their cottage and the big house next door.

'DAD!' she yelled.

The groaning stopped.

She heard a creak and a shuffling sound from across the narrow landing. A shape appeared at the door.

'What's the matter?'

'There's something out there.' Emily could hardly get the words out. 'Or inside. It's in the house. I think it's a tiger.'

'Give me a break, Em.' Dad's voice was croaky and cranky all at once. 'There's nothing to worry about.'

'There *is*. Look. But don't let it see you.'

He climbed up the ladder and lifted the curtain with one finger. 'I can't see anything. It's just your imagination, as usual.'

'I saw it, I swear. And I heard it, right *there*.' She pointed at the wall. 'Call the police.'

'How could it be out there and in here at the same time? Go back to sleep, Em.' He climbed down and went back to his room.

But Emily knew what she'd seen, what she'd heard. She'd have to stay awake. Keep guard.

After the funeral, she'd been sent every week to see

a woman with purple plaits and glasses that made her eyes look bigger than they really were. She was kind and spoke in a soft, inviting voice, asking Emily to talk about how she felt.

'Scared,' Emily had said.

Of what?

She couldn't say. Of everything.

Since Mum had died, she had felt as though something was following her – a huge, faceless monster that wanted to catch her and make her cry. It knew where she was because the emptiness inside her called to it. But every time she opened her mouth to talk about it, she felt like she was in a lift that was dropping too fast.

She had that feeling now. She had to hide.

Listening carefully to make sure Dad was settled in his room again, she crept down the ladder, dragging her panda blanket with her. *There are no monsters in here,* she told herself firmly as she pushed back the door beneath the bed. *Only the one outside.*

The door slid open jerkily, revealing a dark space just the right size for hiding in. She tucked herself in and tried to stay awake. But soon her eyes began to close, and for the first time in six months, it wasn't Mum's face she saw as she drifted into sleep.

It was a much wilder one.

2

The sounds weren't right. Home sounds should be the *clunk* and *whirr* of the central heating coming on, the outside hum of traffic in the street.

Today, it was shouting.

'Emily? EMILY!'

What had she done now? How could she have got into trouble while she was asleep?

She could also hear an engine and a funny sound like lots of little hooves trotting, and a dog barking, but it was all muffled. And *why* was all this going on when everything was still pitch-black?

Then the sliding door was wrenched back and light flooded in.

'What are you doing in there?' demanded Dad. 'I couldn't find you. I didn't know where you were.'

It was all a bit much for Emily. She couldn't remember why she was sleeping in a cupboard either.

Barely awake, she allowed Dad to lift her out. He smelled of the strong disinfectant soap he washed his hands with at the vet surgery. She pressed her ear to his chest so she could share the strong thud of his heart, but he dumped her on the bed with a grunt.

'Em, you're getting much too heavy for this.'

With a sigh, she sat up and pulled back the curtain, half hoping to see the beast from last night so she could prove to Dad that she hadn't been lying. Instead, a flock of sheep was squeezing along the lane, a brown-and-white dog streaking here and there, nipping at their heels. A boy on a quad bike rode behind them, waving a stick and shouting. He looked a couple of years older than Emily, though it was hard to tell because his thick brown hair fell down over his face.

She rapped on the window. The boy looked up, scowled and looked away again, shouting something at the dog.

'Charming!' said Emily.

A voice drifted up the stairs. 'Anyone home? The door was unlocked so I came in.' It was a man's voice, quite posh, breaking into a rumbling cough.

'Does nobody knock in this place?' muttered Dad. 'Em, get dressed before you come down.'

Emily waited a minute or two, then padded down

the stairs after him, still wearing her pyjamas. She sat halfway down. A saggy green sofa slouched against the wall below. Since there was no handrail on the staircase, it was easy to dangle her legs over the edge and plop straight on to it.

'Emily!' Dad snapped.

Not fair. She wasn't doing anything!

An old man with grey whiskers bristling out of his red cheeks waited at the bottom of the stairs, framed by the open door. A wiry Jack Russell stood behind him, sniffing at something on the edge of the path.

'Underwood?' the man boomed, seizing Dad's hand and pumping it up and down. 'Hardacre.' This sounded like a code that spies used to greet each other. 'Everything in order here?'

'Yes, yes, I'm Matt Underwood.' Dad managed to pull his hand away. 'So you're Rufus Hardacre? Your daughter is the vet I'm replacing, isn't she? The one who's gone to Africa? You live next door, don't you? Thanks so much for letting us have your cottage.'

'May as well see it used,' said Rufus. 'Don't want the mice to take over the place.'

'Mice?' Emily jumped up. She wasn't scared of mice, but that didn't mean she wanted them scurrying up her legs when she wasn't even properly dressed.

'Jumpy, is she?' Rufus harrumphed. 'Too many oats. Makes them frisky.'

'I'm not a *horse*,' said Emily. 'I saw a tiger last night.'

Rufus looked at her blankly, then turned to Dad and handed him a leaflet. 'Hope I can count on your support, Underwood, hmm?'

'What is it?' Emily reached out and Dad passed her the leaflet.

No Lynx in Littendale, it said in shouty red capitals. *Save our stock.*

In the very centre of the leaflet was a photo of the beast.

'Of course!' Dad slapped his forehead. 'The Lynx Link. I should have remembered. Em, that must be what you saw, you lucky thing.'

'A Link Slink?' Emily hadn't heard of that before.

'The *Lynx Link,*' Dad said carefully. 'It's a wildlife group that has set some lynx free into the wild. It's called rewilding. You know what a lynx is, right? A big cat.'

Did all dads do that? Ask a question and then answer it right there and then, without giving you the chance to think about it?

'You mean there are wild beasts just wandering around the countryside?' Emily shuddered. 'And there are no fences or anything to keep them in?'

'Exactly.' Rufus looked at Emily properly for the first time. 'It's an outrage. I think you and I might become good friends, young lady, if you continue to talk such common sense.'

'It was in your house last night,' she said. 'I heard it.'

'Emily...' Dad warned.

'It *was*. It made a sort of wailing noise.'

Rufus frowned, his bushy eyebrows almost meeting in the middle. 'That'll be my Jacky.' He nodded towards the Jack Russell, who gave a sharp yap at the sound of his name. 'The old boy does like to make a fuss over nothing.'

'He sounded so sad,' said Emily. 'I feel sorry for him. Shall I come round and see him sometime? I could play with him. I'm good with animals – everyone says so. Don't they, Dad?'

Rufus's face relaxed into a chuckle. 'Then maybe you should become a vet, like your father. Like my Katie.' He pressed his lips together and looked at the ground. 'Africa is such a blasted long way away. Jacky misses her. I'm sure he wouldn't mind a playmate now and again.'

'As I was *about* to say,' Dad cut in, as though Emily had never spoken, 'the lynx don't need fences.' Rufus scowled as Dad went on. 'They're no danger to anyone. The adults are fitted with radio tracking collars, so they can't just wander off.'

Stop it, thought Emily. Rufus's face was getting redder and redder.

'I think it's a great idea to release them into the wild. They'll keep down the deer and rabbit populations, and mainly they keep to themselves.'

'Not so.' Rufus slapped the wall so hard a tiny piece of plaster fell off. 'What about my pheasants, hmm? They'd make a nice meal for a lynx. And the farmers don't want them either – too risky when there are lambs around.'

Dad shook his head. 'They won't take lambs. Not if there are plenty of rabbits.'

'If they're big enough to take down a deer, they're big enough to rip the throat out of a sheep,' roared Rufus.

Or a girl, thought Emily.

Dad planted his hands on his hips. 'I don't mean to be rude, but…'

Rufus butted in like an angry stag. 'I'm sure we *can* count on your support, Underwood. Especially since you're living in my cottage, hmm?'

There was a moment's silence. Dad clenched and unclenched his fists.

'Of course,' he said at last.

3

'Are you *sure* they won't come out during the day?' said Emily. The air outside was so cold it nipped the back of her throat and made her cough. Her breath huffed out in white clouds.

'They prefer twilight and darkness,' said Dad, wrapping a scarf round his neck. 'They're very shy – in fact, some Native American myths used to call the lynx *Keeper of Secrets*. Now, which way? Left or right?'

Emily looked both ways. A few houses were scattered along the road to the right. A handwritten sign hung on the stone wall opposite, pointing to the village. To the left, a track with grass down the middle led past a farm. She could hear the clank of buckets and the low complaint of cows.

'Left,' she said, clapping her gloved hands together.

Dad's phone rang. It had a ringtone like a sheep baaing. He thought it was funny but it confused people sometimes, especially when he was visiting a farm. But she was glad that he'd kept it, even though he found so few things funny these days. It was a reminder that the real Dad was still in there somewhere.

He patted his pockets until he found his phone and peered at the screen.

'Nana Godwin,' he said, holding it out. 'She'll want to speak to you first.'

Emily pressed it to her ear. 'Nana?'

'Hello, pumpkin, how are you?'

She never knew what to say when people asked her that question. It was far too complicated and she didn't know the answer herself.

'Okay, I suppose,' she said. 'It's a bit weird here.'

'Weird?' Nana's Scottish burr rolled down the phone, spiky and comforting, like thistles and shortbread. 'In what way weird?'

'Just...' How to explain? 'The house is cold and it smells funny. My bed has a big cupboard under it and there are some wild cats...'

'Wild cats?' Nana said, sounding surprised. 'It sounds like Scotland to me. Plenty of wild cats up there.'

'Yes, but not right outside your house.'

There was a pause, a wet smacking noise, and Emily knew that Nana was removing one of her favourite minty sweets from her cheek to give Emily her full attention.

'It's bound to feel strange at first, pumpkin. Change is never easy, you know.'

'I know. I wish you were here with us. Six months is such a long time to be away from home.'

Nana Godwin's sigh breezed in Emily's ear. 'Your dad just needed to get away for a while. So many memories, especially at this time of year. I'll be there on Christmas Eve. Only a few days to wait, then you can show me these blessed wild cats and I'll sort them out for you.'

Emily's shoulders relaxed; she hadn't realised she'd been shrugging them up around her ears. Nana was right. It wasn't long to wait.

Dad was reaching out for the phone and pointing at his chest.

'Got to go, Nana,' said Emily. 'Dad wants to talk to you.'

'You take care now,' said Nana. 'Lots of love.' She blew a kiss in Emily's ear and Emily blew one back before handing the phone to Dad. Her toes were beginning to freeze and she hopped from one foot to the other to try to warm them up.

'You go and explore a bit,' said Dad. 'I need to speak to Nana.'

Emily didn't need telling twice. She was drawn to the farm like a bee to a bright flower. Most people didn't like the smell of farms, but she loved it. Warm animals and sweet hay. She didn't even mind the muck.

This must be where that boy lived – the scowly one on the quad bike, with the sheep. She hovered at the gate, peering in. Sometimes, when Dad let her go with him on farm visits, there would be a litter of kittens or a fat puppy, wriggling and wagging its tail. But not this one.

The brown-and-white dog raced up to her, lips peeled back, snarling and snapping, darting and growling at her.

'Streak! Get back here.' It was the boy, dressed in a blue boiler suit and hiking boots, crossing the yard with a bucket in his hand. He didn't look any friendlier close up. Behind him trotted a toddler – a small, curly-haired boy in a matching suit and a pair of bright-green wellies with frog faces on the toes. A plump woman, her hair escaping from a badly tied bun, was hanging sheets on a washing line, ducking in and out between them. *Not much point*, Emily thought, *they'll be frozen stiff by lunchtime.*

The dog, Streak, slunk away into a tumbledown

shed. Emily could see an ancient red tractor in there, its paint peeling, sitting among piles of old fertiliser bags and broken bits of fencing. The whole place looked as though it might collapse in a strong wind.

'Em?' Dad shouted from the cottage door. He waved his phone. 'Might be a while. You can go down the lane but come back in ten minutes or so.' He ducked back inside.

Emily stood uncertainly at the farm gate, shoving a stick around in the mud with her toe. She didn't really want to go down the lane on her own, although she was used to walking to school by herself. It was different here because that … that *beast* was about. Dad *had* said it was safe. Did she believe him? He said a lot of things that weren't true. Like when Mum was in the hospital, wired up to all those tubes and beeping machines. *She'll be okay*, he had said, over and over again.

She snatched up the stick and swiped the air with it, enjoying the vicious *swish* it made. If that dog – or the Link Slink – came near her again, she would give it more than it bargained for.

'Take *that*,' she said, smacking the open gate, 'and *that*.'

A ferocious barking started up from the tractor shed. Emily ran.

There wasn't much to look at down the lane. Lots of half-dead nettles, brambles and some other plants she didn't recognise.

'Come!' said a small voice behind her. Emily turned, and there was the toddler, curls bouncing as he waddled along the road. 'Fump come,' he said.

'Er ... yes, fump come.' Whatever that meant. She wasn't sure what to do. Was he allowed on to the road? Probably not. She tried to shoo him back towards the farm gate, but he didn't want to go.

'Fump come!' he wailed, his face crumpling.

What was he talking about? 'Ssh, don't cry,' she said. 'Go home.'

'No home, no home. Fump come.'

Emily tried to pick him up, but he screamed and wriggled.

'Okay, stay there.'

She put him down and set off along the lane again, chopping the heads off nettles with her stick. In the distance, she heard the rising hum of a car engine. She looked back to check that the little boy was safely at the side, but he was walking in the middle of the lane.

'Car!' Emily waved her arms madly at him. He waved back, a beaming smile on his chubby face.

The car was still coming, moving fast.

'Get off the road,' shouted Emily, hurrying back.

His smile disappeared and he tried to run away from her, but he staggered and fell, sprawled across the grass strip.

She broke into a run, her breath like a steam train. Glancing over her shoulder, she could see a bright red car. The driver's head was bobbing in time to the thump and thud of music.

He hadn't seen; he hadn't heard.

4

Emily threw herself at the little boy. She grabbed him and rolled over to the side of the lane. The car skidded to a halt. There was a yell from the farmyard, and pounding footsteps.

Emily stared up at the sky, at a tiny smudge of blue among the clouds, as though someone had smeared a dirty window with their thumb. The music was still thumping from the car speakers. It made her head thump as well.

'I didn't touch you.' The driver got out of the car and peered down at her. He was a teenager, his head shaved and his mouth sulky. 'Look, the bumper stopped right by your head.'

'Granger, you stupid, stupid idiot,' screamed a voice. 'Haven't I told you before about speeding down this lane?'

It was the woman from the washing line. She

19

leaned down to scoop up the toddler and peppered him with kisses all over, even on his whiffy bum.

'Are you all right? Can you sit up?' The woman grabbed Emily's hand. She had flour all down her front. 'You must come inside and let me call someone. *After* I've reported this to the police.'

Emily allowed herself to be helped up. The woman glared at Granger, whose eyes looked everywhere except back at her.

'Been poaching again, have you?' She nodded towards the back of the car. Emily peeked in and saw a pair of birds, their feathers like rich jewels on the grubby grey seat covers. A shotgun lay beside them, broken across the middle, and a box of red cylinders with metal ends, some of them spilling out across the seat. 'Those pheasants belong to Rufus.'

'No, they don't,' growled Granger. 'I found them dead on the road, didn't I? Must've been knocked down by a car.'

'*Your* car, most likely. Tell you what, hand over those gun cartridges and I won't call the police ... *this* time.'

Granger rolled his eyes. 'Get lost.'

'I mean it.' The woman held out her palm.

Granger spat into the grass and swore a bit more,

but at last he did as he was told and handed over the box of red cylinders. He got back in his car and screeched away, music thumping louder than ever.

✿

The farmhouse kitchen was like a jumble sale. The woman had to shift all kinds of things so that Emily could sit down: newspapers, balls of wool, pieces of Lego and a bundle of letters saying *FINAL DEMAND* in red. She put them on a spare chair, with the box of gun cartridges. A chocolate cake sat on a plate in the middle of the table and Emily's mouth watered. She and Dad had eaten a good breakfast of eggs on toast, but there was always room for cake.

The scowly boy sat opposite her, his hands wrapped around a steaming mug. He glowered at Emily from beneath his fringe.

'Nessie and Bean are at school,' explained the woman. 'Dibs should be there too, but his dad had an accident on the farm and he's in hospital, so we really need Dibs here to take care of things, since we can't afford...'

'Mu-um.' Dibs glared at her. 'That's *our* business.'

The woman ignored him. 'I'm Sal, by the way. And that's Flump.' She pointed at the toddler, who pulled

21

one of the red cylinders out of the box and rolled it across the tabletop.

'NO!' She grabbed it from him and stuffed it back into the box. 'Dibs, take these, will you? Lock them in Dad's gun cabinet.'

Flump began to wail, so Sal gave him a red crayon instead. She went to the sink to wash her hands, then picked up a canister of icing sugar and began to shake it over the cake.

Flump. So that's what he was saying out in the lane. What a strange name. The others were just as weird. Nessie – that sounded like the Loch Ness Monster – and Bean and … *Dibs*.

She glanced at the tall clock standing in the corner. Better go soon. Dad would blow his top if he couldn't find her again. But it was so much cosier here than in the dreary old cottage.

Five minutes, she promised herself. *Then I'll go.*

'Not seen you round here before,' Sal went on as she put the icing sugar down and licked her finger. 'You here on holiday?'

Emily couldn't imagine anyone coming to Littendale for a holiday. 'My dad's a vet. He's here for six months while the other vet's away. She's gone to Africa to look after giraffes. We're staying in Badger Cottage and I'm going to school here after Christmas.'

'Not one of the lynx lot, are you?' said Dibs.

What was the right answer? Were the 'lynx lot' the ones who wanted the big cats, or the ones who didn't?

She was distracted when Sal carried a tray of biscuits over to an old-fashioned Aga that had two ovens, one above the other.

That was the last time Emily had seen Mum – standing by the oven at home, pulling out a tray of biscuits and putting it on the side to cool. Her throat felt tight, as though something was caught there.

Sal opened a lower door. 'Oops, wrong one.'

Emily blinked.

There was a kitten in the oven.

5

Sal closed the oven door again. The kitten was still inside.

'Wait!' shouted Emily. 'There's a kitten in the oven.'

Sal smiled and blew a stray hair out of her face. 'It's an orphan. In there to keep warm, since it has no mum. Poor thing was a bit old for kittens, and she died giving birth. Only managed to push this one out, and it's a right scrap of nothing.'

She opened the door again and beckoned Emily over for a peep. 'Don't fret, love. It won't cook. Bottom oven just stays nice and warm.'

Emily crouched down, the warmth flushing her cheeks. A folded cloth lined the bottom of the oven, and on it lay a tiny tabby kitten with a white tummy. It was fast asleep, but it stirred when Emily stretched out a gentle finger to touch its head.

'Only a couple of weeks old,' said Sal. 'You can feed it if you want.'

'Can I?' All thoughts of the time went out of Emily's head. Sal made her sit down cross-legged and draped a towel across her lap. Then she lifted the kitten out and laid it gently into Emily's cupped hands.

'Show her how to feed it, Dibs,' said Sal. 'I've got to change this stinky nappy and get the washing sorted.' She scooped Flump up, crayon and all, and swept him out of the room.

The kitchen was suddenly silent, except for the ticking clock. It was just Emily and Dibs, and the Aga, which was feeling hotter by the minute. She focused on the kitten, the lightness of it in her hands, like a glove full of twigs. When it wriggled, she could feel all the bones moving beneath its skin.

'Why are you called Dibs?' she asked, just as Dibs said, 'Better show you, then.'

They looked at each other. Emily waited for his answer.

Dibs growled, 'Do you want to feed the kitten, or don't you?'

Emily nodded. Let him be a rudey-pants. She didn't care. And he still hadn't put those cartridges away; he'd just left them on the table.

He showed her how to suck some milk into a syringe and feed it, drop by drop, into the kitten's

25

eager mouth. When it wouldn't take any more, he lifted it from Emily's hands and put it back into the oven.

'You're quite good with animals,' he said begrudgingly. 'Want to see the rest of the place?'

'I can't, I...' Emily's eyes flickered towards the clock. Maybe another five minutes wouldn't hurt. After all, she'd hear Dad from here if he shouted for her.

It seemed colder than ever outside after the warmth of the kitchen. Streak sat by the gate, ears pricked, watching the road intently.

'Hey, lass,' called Dibs.

Streak's tail began to beat against the ground, but she never took her eyes off the road.

'Funny, that.' Dibs shook his head. 'She used to be all over me – right friendly, like. She's still a great dog, but she's gone off a bit. Sort of snappy.'

A massive bang split the sky, sending up a shower of cawing rooks from the trees nearby. Streak flashed across the yard into the shed near the gate, where she hid beneath the old red tractor.

'See what I mean?' Dibs led the way to the shed as the birds squawked and circled up above. 'That'll be Rufus out shooting pheasants. Streak never used to be scared of that.'

26

Streak had dug a hole under the tractor and was hiding there. The entrance to the hole was littered with flakes of red paint that had peeled off the tractor. It looked quite pretty, as though the dog had decorated it for Christmas.

'It's because I'm so greedy,' said Dibs.

'She's hiding because you're greedy?' That made no sense. Surely he didn't steal the dog's food? There looked to be plenty of better stuff on offer in the kitchen.

'No. Why they call me Dibs. Whenever there's a pie or something, I always say, "I'm the oldest. I get first dibs."'

Emily frowned. Why did people around here speak in such riddles?

His face relaxed into a proper smile for the first time. 'It's what we say round here. It means I get first go – first choice. Biggest piece of pie.'

'So it's a nickname?'

Dibs nodded. 'Littlun's called Flump because that's the noise he makes whenever he falls down on his backside. *Phhhlump.*' A laugh got caught in his throat, as though it didn't happen very often.

'So what should my nickname be?' Emily leaned back against the tractor, sending another shower of red flakes on to the soil below. 'My actual name is Emily.'

Dibs pretended to stroke an imaginary beard. 'Well, you did a bit of superhero stuff this afternoon, rescuing our Flump from that car, so how about Soup?'

'Soup?'

'Short for superhero.'

'You can't call me *Soup*!'

'Why not? My brother's called Bean.'

'Why Bean?'

Emily ducked out of the tractor shed, as Dibs led her between the outbuildings to a gate with fields beyond it. She had to pick her way carefully through the piles of wet straw and muck. Everything seemed to need fixing around here, and Dibs's boiler suit was patched and stitched all over. They passed a grassy patch by the farmhouse with the washing line where Sal's sheets hung lifeless in the cold air.

'No, don't tell me. Let me guess – he's really fast at running so he's called Bean. Runner Bean.'

'Good guess, but wrong. Try again.'

'He eats loads of beans so he's always farting?'

This time a proper laugh burst out of Dibs's nose. 'Wrong, all wrong.'

He stopped at the far end of the yard, before the field gate, and nodded towards a long, low cowshed with one side open to the yard. Half a dozen black-

and-white cows, barred in by a feeding trough full of silage, eyed her lazily and kept on chewing. 'When he were a little kid, Mum would always make him go to the toilet before he sat down for his tea. Otherwise he'd need to go, like, in the middle of it. So after a while he'd run in *before* tea and shout, "Been!" because he'd already been. Geddit? Been ... Bean.'

Dibs frowned. He bent over and peered at something in the mud. He muttered a swear word that Emily wasn't even allowed to hear on TV, let alone use. 'Look at that!'

There, in the smeared mud and muck outside the cowshed, was a footprint. A paw print, to be precise, but much bigger than any she'd seen before.

'What are you looking at?' Sal came out with yet another basket full of washing, Flump tottering after her.

'This,' said Dibs grimly, beckoning her over and poking at the paw print.

'Is it a dog? Bigger than Streak.'

Dibs shook his head. 'No claw prints. They're sheathed. Which means...'

'It's a cat,' said Emily.

Dibs said, 'Not a cat. Not a normal one, anyway. Look at the *size* of it.'

Emily held her hand above the print. It was easily

the size of her palm, with four distinct pads. 'The Link Slink,' she breathed. 'It's been here, too.'

'What do you mean?' asked Dibs.

'I saw one last night,' she said. 'A ... a lynx.'

'What? Where?'

'In the lane, right outside my bedroom window.'

'No,' Sal burst out. 'They can't come here. I won't have it. Lambing's only a few weeks away. We can't afford to lose any.'

Emily stared at the paw print. The beast had been here, right where she was standing. What if it was hiding inside the cowshed, those golden eyes narrowed in the dark, waiting to jump out on them? Maybe that's why Streak was going berserk all of a sudden, yelping and barking.

The farmyard gate creaked. Streak shot out of the tractor shed and Emily whirled round to look, her stomach somersaulting.

Dad.

Relief made her legs rubbery, but not for long. 'What time is it?' she hissed at Dibs. 'How long have I been here?' But he was already striding up to the gate.

Instinctively, Emily ducked behind one of the sheets on the washing line, breathing in the homely scent of fabric conditioner. She peeped around the edge. Dibs was squaring up to Dad with his hands on his hips.

'Who are you?' His voice had turned sulky again. 'What do you want?'

Dad was peering at Streak, who had something frothy round her muzzle. 'What've you been into, eh, girl?' he said, trying to get a closer look. But Streak backed away, snarling and licking her lips at the same time. Dad sighed and straightened up, just in time to catch sight of Emily as she ducked back behind the damp sheet.

'*Emily*,' he roared, as though she too was a disobedient dog. 'Here. Now.'

And she had no choice but to slink towards him, imaginary tail between her legs, growling inside.

6

Next morning, Dad was still in a bad mood.

'You stay with me today, young lady,' he said. 'I'm not letting you out of my sight.'

'I'm not a little kid.'

'If you want me to treat you responsibly, then you have to behave responsibly,' said Dad.

There was a cobbled courtyard behind the cottage with a stone wall and a wide metal gate leading out on to the lane. Emily had no choice but to hang about there all morning while Dad chopped firewood and stacked it in a tightly jammed pile behind an old outhouse.

'What's in here?' She tugged at the outhouse door, which opened with a grinding scrape.

'Outside toilet,' grunted Dad, lifting another heavy chunk of wood.

There was nothing in there now except a piece of pipe sticking out of the wall and a whole heap of spiders. Emily went in and pulled the door shut. With no window, it was completely dark.

Dad yanked the door open.

'Stop doing that, will you?' he snapped. 'That disappearing thing. You have to start being sensible. I have to *work*, Emily, I have to get things done – all the things that Mum did as well, but there's no one else...' His voice cracked. He lifted his shirt and rubbed at his face with it.

Emily didn't know where to look, so she dusted spiders' webs off her jeans. 'I can be sensible.'

'You have to *prove* it, Em.'

Dad lifted the axe and was about to drive it into a log when a grinning woman, her arms full of brown paper bags, shouldered the gate open and came in. Her hair was a fiery curtain around her shoulders, and even though her face looked a bit older than Dad's, she was dressed like a child in a mossy-green cardigan, a rainbow-coloured skirt, thick tights patterned with leaves, and a pair of red leather shoes that fastened with gigantic flowers.

'You're here!' she said, as though it was the most exciting thing that had happened to her in a long time. 'Welcome to Littendale. I'm Josie.' She bobbed

33

into a half-curtsey. 'Here to help with anything you need.'

Dad rubbed his chin, bristles rasping against his fingers. 'Thank you, that's very kind, but we can take care of ourselves, can't we, Em?'

Josie's smile dimmed. 'Oh. Well, if you do need anything, I'll be in my studio for the rest of the day.'

'Studio?' asked Emily.

Josie pointed at a low building tucked behind the big house. Its walls were painted white and the roof was a wavy metal sea. 'There. I'm an artist.'

'Can I see?'

'Not now, Em. We're busy,' said Dad. His voice had that heaviness that Emily felt when she was just too tired to be polite and speak nicely to people. He pressed two fingers against his forehead, as though he was trying to rub away an ache. He was always so angry these days.

'How about later?' said Josie.

'Please! Just…' Dad bit back whatever he had been about to say. 'Leave us alone.'

He hadn't been like this before. Everyone had brought their sick pets to him because he was so kind and patient. Sometimes it felt like Emily had lost two parents instead of one, and she was left with this irritable stranger who looked like Dad and talked like him, but who had locked the real one away somewhere.

Emily would go and rescue him if she knew where he was.

Josie swallowed hard, obviously trying her hardest to be nice even though Dad was being such a bad-tempered old troll, like the one who lived under a bridge and shouted at goats.

'I don't know what it's like where you live,' she said, in the same kind of voice that Emily's teacher used when one of the naughty-boys-who-couldn't-help-it was misbehaving, 'but that's not how we do things around here.' She spun round, her skirt flaring round her knees, and marched into her studio.

Emily wondered whether she should run after Josie and explain, but she couldn't think what she would say without having to go into the whole story, so her feet stayed rooted to the cobbles.

Dad stared at the ground, breathing heavily.

'I'll apologise later,' he muttered. Then he swung the axe into the wood, splitting it in two.

🐾

Lunch was a silent affair over bowls of tomato soup and brown bread in the little kitchen at the back of the cottage. Emily wasn't hungry. She pushed away her bowl still half-full, and began to gather all the bread crumbs with her finger, pushing them into a neat mound.

There was a tap at the back door.

Dad and Emily exchanged glances, but before either of them could get up to open it, Josie stepped in. Behind her, a man wearing a black fleece and a woolly hat with a bobble on the top peeped round the door. He had rectangular glasses and a kind face.

'This is Andy,' said Josie, a fresh smile firmly fixed on her face. 'I saw Rufus and he said he'd told you about the Lynx Link.' She folded her arms. 'So I thought you needed to know the *other* side of the story.'

Dad got up and went to the sink, where he clattered pots and pans loudly. Wasn't he supposed to be apologising?

Josie's eyes flickered towards him, but she kept on speaking. 'Andy works for the Lynx Link and he's offered to take you into the forest to see if you can spot one.'

'No.' Emily pressed herself back in her chair. 'I don't want to.'

The clattering stopped. 'Actually, that's a great idea.' Dad turned to face the visitors, the soup pan in his hand dripping water on to the floor. 'Perhaps it will get this "beast" nonsense out of my daughter's head. And…' He stared down at the pan as though it was the most interesting thing he'd seen in a long time. 'I need to say sorry. For my behaviour earlier.'

'Don't mention it.' Josie waved the apology away.

'It was very rude of me.' He looked at her like a puppy that's been caught weeing behind the sofa. 'Can we begin again?' He held out his hand, still damp from the washing-up water.

Josie shook it heartily. 'I think that's an excellent idea.'

No one seemed to be taking any notice of Emily. 'I don't *want* to,' she said again.

Josie crouched in front of her, which made Emily feel boxed in, so she stood up abruptly, the chair leg screeching across the floor.

'There's a kitten,' said Josie.

'A lynx kitten?'

'That's right,' said Andy. 'It's one we have to keep a special eye on. Born very late, in June, after the mother lost her first litter.'

June. In her mind's eye, Emily saw Mum again, standing by the oven with her last tray of biscuits.

'I'm just popping out to the shop for some icing sugar,' she had said. 'Do you want to come?'

Emily hadn't wanted to. She and Dad were making a model for a school project and they were just at a tricky bit.

'I'll take the car.' Mum had planted a kiss on Emily's forehead. 'I'll be back before you know it.'

Only she wasn't. After the accident, the police had found a bag of sugar in the car, split open, spilling its sweetness all across the mangled dashboard.

A panicky feeling rose up inside Emily, as though a bottomless hole had opened up in the kitchen floor and her feet were balancing either side of it. She fought for something else to think about, some words – any words.

'Why?' she gasped. 'Why do you have to keep a special eye on it?'

'Because it's very young to survive such a cold winter,' said Andy.

'Shouldn't it be a … a cub?' said Emily. 'It's a big cat. Lions and tigers have cubs.' She was gabbling now; she couldn't get her breath properly.

Josie frowned slightly. Dad moved closer. Andy didn't seem to notice anything.

'No one can make up their minds,' he laughed. 'Cats have kittens, but lions and tigers have cubs. But a lynx is in a different family than lions and tigers, so most experts call a young lynx a kitten.'

'Will we see it?' The shaky feeling was beginning to pass. Emily dropped heavily into her chair.

'I can't promise anything,' said Andy, and Emily didn't know whether to be disappointed or relieved.

🐾

Half an hour later, she was walking through the forest, sandwiched between Andy and Dad. She half wished that Josie had come with them too. She might be a stranger, but there was safety in numbers, wasn't there? A gunshot sounded, and Emily dropped back, to be closer to Dad.

'What if we get shot?'

'We won't.'

'How do you know?'

'Because they're shooting upwards into the sky at the pheasants that fly over them. Unless you decide to climb a tree and launch yourself out of it in front of their guns, it's highly unlikely that you'll get shot today.' Dad winked at her; he seemed in a better mood since he'd apologised to Josie. 'Honestly, Em, it's fine.'

Emily stayed quiet for a while, then: 'I thought you said the lynx only came out at night?'

Dad shrugged. 'Apparently when the weather gets

colder, they get more active during the day. That's what Andy said.'

The trees were silvery against the damp, dank ground. Pieces of bark peeled off like bits of dead skin. They made Emily think of skeletons. Andy led them on, this way and that, until Emily was completely lost. If he decided to abandon them for any reason, they might never find their way back. A twig snapped. Emily froze.

'What's that?' she whispered.

'Only a deer,' said Dad, in the voice he used for calming nervy cats. 'Look.'

All three of them stood still as a deer, freckled with white spots, stepped carefully between the ghostly trunks, sniffing the air. If the deer wasn't afraid, then surely ...

Suddenly, it bounded away, leaping over a bramble bush, catching its leg against a thorny briar. Emily saw the panic in its eyes as it struggled before managing to get free.

Something had startled it. She sidled up close to Dad and slid her hand into his. He gave her the surprised-but-pleased look he wore when she made him a homemade card for his birthday and squeezed her hand tightly, before letting go and striding on.

Andy was walking more slowly now, casting glances in every direction. A breeze lifted some dry leaves into a whirling, crackling dance and Emily's skin prickled. She realised that she was at the back, unprotected against sudden pounces, and she scuttled forward between Dad and Andy again.

'Shhh. Get down.' Andy motioned with his hand.

Emily and Dad dropped to the ground as though they *had* been shot. They lay on the ground, propped up on their elbows behind a decaying log with a huge fungus growing out of it, like a gnarly ear. Andy held up his hand, palm outwards, telling them *stay there*, and he crept further down the path.

'I don't like it here,' Emily whimpered, wrinkling her nose at the fungus.

'Don't be silly,' said Dad. 'This is the experience of a lifetime.'

For him, maybe. Not her. What if the beast came round behind them while Andy was ahead, and sank its claws into their skulls? A scuffle in the leaves made Emily whip round.

Just a blackbird. It exploded into the air in a flurry of wings, shrilling its alarm call.

Dad nudged her. Andy was crouching behind a rock, pointing urgently at something off to his right. The light filtering through the trees was dappled there, moving and changing all the time, making it look like a…

'Kitten,' breathed Emily and Dad at the same time.

It was lying by a rocky outcrop, tearing at a piece of red meat and grey fur. Much smaller than the lynx Emily had seen in the lane – but still a lot bigger than any pet cat she'd ever seen – it had the same tasselled ears and streaked fur. A sudden beam of sunlight raked its back, highlighting all the shades of chestnut and gold, the smudges of glossy black. Its eyes and ears looked too big for its face. A leaf bowled past it in the breeze and its paw shot out playfully to pin it down.

'It's so *cute*,' Emily murmured. How could she be scared of something that looked like a bigger version of the kitten in Sal's oven?

But then she went rigid again as an adult lynx came stepping carefully through the undergrowth, flicking moisture from its paws. Its muscles rippled beneath its fur as it leapt on to the rocky outcrop, crouched beside the kitten and licked it behind the ears.

'Mother and six-month-old kitten,' said Andy's voice in Emily's ear, making her jump. He certainly could move silently when he wanted to. 'Just the one. It won't go far from its mother. Still learning to hunt.'

Both mother and kitten flickered their ears and

looked up, right at the log. The mother stood up, golden eyes wide. Two tufts of white fur, edged with black, hung down each side of her jaws, mirroring the pricked ears above. *Beautiful*, whispered Emily's heart. *Dangerous*, her head replied.

'Why is the mother wearing that collar?' she asked.

Andy spoke so quietly it was barely a voice, and Emily had to bend her head really close to hear him.

'Radio tracking collar. We monitor her movements so we can tell exactly where she goes. Kitten doesn't have one yet, but we'll put one on it in the spring.'

The kitten was on its feet, the remains of the rabbit dangling from its mouth.

'Down!' hissed Andy, and they all pressed their faces against the mossy ground.

Emily could feel a tiny bug crawling across her face and she longed to flick it off, but she didn't dare move. A couple of minutes passed with no sound but the little panting breaths of people trying to be silent. But when Emily lifted her head to peer over the top of the log again, both the lynx had gone. Someone was standing right where they had been.

Granger.

'What's he doing here?' she hissed, and the sound made him look in her direction. He didn't look happy to see her.

'He's doing an apprenticeship with the Lynx Link,' said Andy cheerfully, getting to his feet. 'Learning the ropes. Protecting wildlife is an important skill. We need to pass it on.'

Emily thought of the pheasants in the back seat of Granger's car, of the gun and the cartridges beside them, but she said nothing.

They said goodbye and thanks to Andy once he'd led them back to the lane. The chimneys of Badger Cottage were visible so they hadn't been all that lost, not really.

'That was *awesome*.' Dad's face was alight, all traces of bad temper smoothed away. He nudged Emily. 'Wasn't it?'

Emily knew what she should say. It was amazing, it was epic, wasn't nature wonderful, blah-blah. It was true – it had been exciting to see the lynx, and that kitten was *so* cute, but she couldn't shake off the deep, gnawing fear that chewed at her stomach.

'I'm still scared,' she whispered. 'It's out there in the *day* as well.'

And so was the other beast, the faceless one; the one that made her feel as panicky as that deer caught in the brambles. She felt it in the hollow of her stomach, in the way Dad looked at her, hoping for her to say something – anything – that would let him know she was all right. But she wasn't, and she didn't think she ever would be.

'But don't you think it was beautiful?' he pressed.

She shook her head and said in a small voice, 'I want to go home.' And by that, she meant *home* home, not the dreary dump that was Badger Cottage.

Dad's face closed up again. 'Well, we can't always have what we want, can we?' And he stamped away, kicking up leaves with his big, black boots.

7

'Do I *have* to?' Emily glared at the green door of Josie's studio. To the right of the door, on an old gatepost, sat a stone owl. It guarded a knotty piece of wood with *Welcome* printed on it in bright white paint. The owl didn't look very welcoming. 'I'm perfectly all right staying on my own. Plus you shouldn't leave me with a stranger.'

'She's not a stranger any more,' said Dad. 'She's been kind to us. And I don't want you being on your own too much.' He stopped, palm against the door. 'It's not good to have too much time to brood, especially when we've just got here and you don't really know anyone yet.'

'I know Dibs and Sal and Flump.'

Dad frowned a question.

'At the farm.'

'I think they have their hands full without you

hanging around as well. Besides, they have jobs to do.'

'I could help.' Emily thought longingly of the warm, cluttered kitchen and the banter over the table. And she wanted to see the kitten again.

'Maybe tomorrow. For now, you can hang out with Josie.'

'Why can't I stay with you?'

'I have to go and meet everyone else at the surgery. I'll be starting straight after Christmas. To be honest, I think you should do the same – meet everyone at the school now, before the holidays.'

'No. Not yet.' She didn't want to be the New Girl, stared at. Mum would have made it seem like an adventure; she would have squeezed Emily's hand before she went in, and she would have been waiting at the gate afterwards to hear all about it. Emily wouldn't have felt so alone.

'Then Josie it is. Anyway, it's all arranged. I spoke to her earlier and she's looking forward to having you.'

Inside, the studio was a cave of colour. Every bit of wall space had a decoration pinned to it. There were bells and hedgehogs, baubles and hearts, glittering spirals and fat gingerbread men stitched from felt.

'Ah, you're here!' Josie appeared through a sliding door, wearing a green tunic dress belted over red tights. She smiled. 'I was thinking you could help me make some decorations.'

Dad gave Josie his phone number, warned Emily to behave and hurried away without looking back.

Josie beckoned her through the door into another room, where holly, ivy and other greenery hung from the wooden beams in the ceiling. A half-finished painting of a lynx stood on an easel. Emily stared it. The lynx was so lifelike it looked as though it could jump from the picture at any second.

'Do you like it?' asked Josie. 'I'm hoping to sell it to the tourists.'

'Tourists? Here?'

'They come to see if they can spot the lynx. It's great for the village – all the shops and cafés do a booming business.'

'But I thought the people in the village didn't want them?'

Josie pulled a face. 'Some do; some don't. Anyway...' She wiped her hands with a rag. 'Would you like to make some decorations for your Christmas tree?'

'We don't have a tree,' said Emily, 'and I'm rubbish at making things.'

'Nonsense. Everyone can make things. You just need the confidence to have a go.'

Emily shook her head. 'I don't feel like it.'

'Tell you what, you can have one of these.' Josie stood on a wobbly stool, unhooked a star from one of the beams and gave it to Emily. It was made of twigs, painted pale green and studded with what looked like huge sugar crystals. A loop of gold thread was attached to the top. 'They say that if you hang a star in your window, it will bring someone home to you.' She looked thoughtful. 'You hang it there and wish for the person you want most of all.'

The studio felt too hot and the beams far too low. The star was spiky in Emily's hand. What did Josie know about anything? She was just a stupid woman dressed as an elf, who spent her days cutting and sticking and painting like some little kid who didn't have anything better to do.

She raced out of the studio, ignoring Josie's cries. As she passed, she knocked the welcome owl off its post. It fell to the ground with a loud crack. She charged into the cottage and up the stairs to her bedroom, where she flung the star against the window as hard as she could, tears pouring down her burning cheeks.

'Stupid woman! Stupid star!' She threw herself on to the panda blanket inside the cupboard, sobbing hard enough to turn herself inside out.

It wasn't long before she heard footsteps hammering up the stairs. Dad burst into the room. She hadn't even bothered to shut the sliding doors, so this time he found her straight away.

'Sweetheart,' he said, gathering her in his arms. 'Josie called me. She didn't mean to... She didn't *know*. I didn't tell her about Mum. She was only trying to help.'

'She gave me ... a star and said ... it would bring ... the person ... I most ... wanted.' Emily could hardly get the words out between gulps.

Dad let his chin fall on to Emily's head. 'It brought me,' he said, hopefully.

Emily paused, her breath coming in great gulps. 'It's Mum I want.'

Dad was silent. 'Look,' he said at last. 'It glows in the dark.' He held out the star, which looked so much smaller in his big hand.

Emily hadn't expected that. It shimmered in the dark cupboard with a pale green glow. But she wouldn't take it.

'Sometimes Mum visits me while I'm asleep,' said Dad, 'in my dreams. Perhaps if you put this under your pillow, she'll do the same for you.'

'No.' She shook her head. 'It won't work.'

'I'll put it there anyway, in case you change your

mind.' Dad lifted her pillow and slid the star underneath.

After he'd gone, Emily shut the cupboard door and lay in the dark for a long while, one hand clutching a handful of panda blanket and the other beneath her pillow, curled around the star.

8

When Emily woke next morning, there was a strange light in the room. Everything sounded oddly silent. She crawled out of the cupboard and climbed on to the bed to open the curtains.

Snow! And not just the feeble sprinkle they used to get in town. Proper, thick, exciting snow … and it was still falling. Fat flakes dawdled from the sky like clumpy feathers, resting on her windowsill, layer upon layer, banking up against the glass.

Dibs came down the lane on his quad bike, with Streak darting here and there behind him as though she was trying to round him up. This time when Emily knocked, he looked up and grinned, standing up on the quad bike and beckoning to her to come down. She didn't need asking twice.

'Dad? Can I go out?' He was sitting at the kitchen table with a steaming mug of tea, staring into space.

'Where to?'

'Just to the farm. I won't go anywhere else, I promise.' It should be safe enough there. Even if a lynx did come looking for her, Dibs would be there, and Streak could put up a decent fight.

'Promise?'

'Cross my heart and hope to die.' The last word hung in the air between them. But Dad smiled.

'Don't do that, Em. Who would keep me on my toes then?'

She flung her arms round his neck and gave him a quick hug. Dad pulled out a hanky and blew his nose hard. 'Coming down with a cold,' he said, and Emily pretended to believe him. 'Tell you what, how about we go and look for a Christmas tree this afternoon?'

Emily's shoulders drooped. 'We haven't got anything to put on it.'

'That's where you're wrong.' Dad reached for a cardboard box on the kitchen bench and shook it under Emily's chin. It was full of Josie's homemade decorations. 'Josie dropped these off to say sorry. She feels terrible, you know.'

Let her, was Emily's first thought. But outside the kitchen window, she could see the snow falling thicker than ever, so she just nodded.

By the time she had bundled herself up in hat,

boots, scarf, gloves and jacket, Dibs was already back at the farm. She could hear the thrum of the quad bike engine beyond the barns. Hovering anxiously at the gate, she peered around to see whether Streak was about.

At times like this, when she was outside, alone, she felt the breath of the faceless monster welling up inside her own body, trying to suffocate her. At one of the counselling sessions, the kind woman with the big glasses had asked her to describe what it felt like, and all she could think of was when she'd got lost in the woods, picking blackberries with Mum. Panic. Not knowing the way. Feeling like something was out there, among the branches, closing in on her... And then she had spotted Mum's bright green coat, run to meet her, and the terror had backed off.

Maybe it had always been there. Only now, Mum wasn't there to keep it away.

She was about to run back to the cottage when Sal came out of the farmhouse with a face like thunder and a long package under her arm, wrapped in an old sack. She loaded it into the back of a Land Rover and slammed the door shut.

'Sal,' called Emily, waving.

A smile forced itself on to Sal's face. 'Morning. Have you come to give us a hand? I'm off to the

54

hospital. Going to see my husband. Dibs'll be glad to see you.'

Emily stepped on to a patch of untouched snow just beyond the gate. Nobody in the whole world had ever stepped on it. She was the first human being to walk there.

'What happened to him? Your husband, I mean.'

Sal sighed. 'Tractor accident. It turned over on him, and the roll bar hadn't been properly fixed. Not enough money. And now that wretched lynx has been back sniffing around here. Someone needs to *do* something.'

'Is it fixed now? The tractor, I mean.' Emily looked at the red tractor sitting in the shed. A drift of snow had blown in there, flecks of red paint dotting it like measles. What if Dibs drove it and the same thing happened to him?

'Not that one – that ancient old thing doesn't work. Should get rid of it, really.' Sal leaned against the Land Rover and shook her head, as though it was all too much to think about. 'Dibs is about somewhere. My sister's indoors keeping an eye on Flump. Nessie and Bean are home from school as well, due to the snow. You should meet them – be good for you to make some more friends, though they're a pair of tearaways. Tell you what, why don't you come in?

They were putting on some hot chocolate when I came out. I don't have to leave for ten minutes and you look as though you could do with warming up.'

Emily trotted eagerly into the welcoming warmth of the farmhouse kitchen. A smiling woman with curly hair had Flump on her lap and was playing a clapping game with him. A girl and a boy were over by the Aga, quarrelling over a saucepan and a bottle of milk. The girl was taller, but only just.

'Nessie and Bean,' said Sal, waving a hand towards them.

'You have to put more milk in that that,' said Nessie. She had thin, mousy plaits and wore a pair of denim dungarees. 'Otherwise it comes out all powdery and it won't froth up.'

'Mum, have we got any marshmallows?' Bean – a smaller, blonder copy of Dibs – looked over his shoulder towards Sal and did a double take when he saw Emily. 'Who's that?'

Dibs came in, stamping his feet, clumps of snow falling all over the floor.

'Soup,' he cried, his face splitting into a smile. 'You're just in time for morning tea. We always stop at this time for a cuppa and a cake.'

Emily loved the way that she was automatically included. Not: 'Would you like a cuppa and a cake?'

He just assumed that she would have some. And it would be rude to refuse, wouldn't it?

She pulled up the same chair as before, draped her coat over the back of it and smiled at Bean. He and Nessie just stared at her while the milk boiled over behind them and spilled all over the Aga.

'Oh, Bean,' said Sal crossly.

'Oh, Bee,' echoed Flump, bouncing up and down on the curly-haired woman's knees.

'And I'm Alison, from the village,' she said. 'Sal's sister.' Emily could see the likeness, now she'd said it – the same smile, the same slightly downturned eyes, only Alison was much thinner than Sal.

'I think there's someone else who would like to see you,' said Dibs with a grin. He went over to the Aga, elbowed Nessie and Bean aside and scooped out the kitten. Even in two days, it had grown. Its eyes were fully open and its ears were pricked up from its head. The tabby stripes had grown darker, making the white splodge on its tummy look like a bright star.

Dibs laid it in Emily's hands and it nestled there as though it was perfectly at home. Its tiny pink tongue darted out and rasped against Emily's skin. It gave the tiniest miaow, little more than a mousy squeak.

'Hungry, I think,' said Dibs, fetching some milk and the syringe.

Emily sat the kitten on the table. 'Is it a boy or a girl?' she asked.

'Boy,' said Sal, hastily putting a clean tea towel beneath the kitten. 'Don't want any accidents, do we?'

'You could give it a name if you want to,' said Dibs.

'*I* wanted to give it a name,' protested Nessie.

'You've named pretty much every kitten we've ever had and you've already been through the alphabet,' said Dibs. 'I bet even you can't come up with a good name beginning with X. Anyway, let Soup do it. She rescued Flump, you know.'

'I agree,' said Sal. 'Let Soup do it.'

Even Sal was using her nickname. Emily felt like the kitten, basking in the warmth of their approval. She wanted to stretch out, roll over and give a happy miaow of her own. If she'd been at home and Mum had been with her, she would have actually done it, and Mum would have laughed and said, 'Happy, my little kitty-cat?'

But not here, not now. If she did that, they would think she was weird and she wanted them to like her as much as she liked them.

'I'll call him Alexander,' she declared.

Nessie snorted. 'Alexander? What kind of a name is that?'

Emily shrugged. 'It's a mighty kind of name

because even though he's small now, he's going to grow into a mighty cat, I just know he is.' She glanced at Nessie. 'And it's got an "X" in it.'

Nessie hid her face in her mug of hot chocolate, but Emily could swear there was a tiny smile behind it.

'Well, I'd better get on over to the hospital,' said Sal. 'Stay as long as you like.'

'I've got jobs to do,' said Dibs. 'Come outside when you're done, Soup. You can give me a hand.'

When the kitten had drunk its fill of milky drops, Emily carefully laid it in the oven and closed the door – almost, but not quite. She huddled into her coat and went outside in search of Dibs, but he was nowhere to be seen. She took a step towards the old tractor for a closer look, but Streak appeared, circling round behind her and nipping at her heels.

'Catch this, Soup!' Dibs appeared around the corner of the cowshed and hurled a snowball. It missed her and smacked into the ground in front of Streak, who erupted into frantic, high-pitched barking and made a dash for the safety of the tractor shed. She sniffed at the red flecks and licked one or two before burrowing into her hole.

'I swear she thinks she's a rabbit,' said Dibs. He went after her and called, 'Come out, you daft thing.'

Streak shot out of the hole, snapping at him. Her muzzle was frothy again, and some of it dripped on to the snow.

'Hey, watch it. It's me!' Dibs looked shaken. 'I don't know what's up with her – she's always been such a friendly dog. Could be she's picking up on all the stress. Mum will get into trouble if she keeps me off school much longer, but she can't do everything on her own.'

Emily inched closer to Dibs. It was so cold out here compared with the warmth of the kitchen. For a while, she had forgotten about the golden-eyed lynx stalking silent-footed through the daylight hours, but now...

'Maybe she's scared.'

'Nah, she's not scared of anything. Not our Streak.'

Emily hadn't really been talking about the dog.

🐾

After lunch, Emily and Dad went to get a Christmas tree.

'Josie says there's a Christmas tree plantation on the other side of the village,' he said. 'You can choose whichever one you want. Oh, and Nana Godwin called.'

60

'Nana Godwin? You should have come to get me.'

'I told her you'd made a new friend already.' Dad looked over his shoulder to reverse the car into the lane. 'She was pleased.'

'But I wanted to speak to her.'

'You can ring her later if you want.' The car wheels spun on the snow, where earlier traffic had packed it flat. 'Tell her we're snowed in.'

'She will be able to get here, won't she?' said Emily, suddenly anxious.

'Nothing will stop Nana Godwin, you know that.' Dad looked into the rear-view mirror and smiled at her. 'And it's still a few days till she comes. This lot will have gone by then.'

It was half past four when they finally chose a tree. Dusk was beginning to ink the sky. Dad dragged the tree into the boot of the car and squashed it down.

'Looks like we might be in for more snow,' he said.

The car headlights picked out streaks of ice glittering in tyre tracks on the lane. Even though Dad drove slowly, the car slid from one side to the other. In the back seat, Emily huddled her knees up to her chin and stared out of the window into the darkening forest. There was still enough light in the sky to see the patches of snow between the tree trunks.

They were about half a mile from Badger Cottage

when she spotted something lying on the ground in between two trees – a sort of heap, like someone had dumped an old fur coat there – and a dark shape moving about close by, pushing at it.

'Dad...?'

'Let me concentrate, Em. There's black ice on the road.'

'But I think there's...'

'Emily! What did I say?'

Emily pressed her nose right up against the window as she strained to see better, willing the light to hold out.

Because she could swear that was a lynx lying there, a scarlet stain spreading from it across the untouched beauty of the snow.

9

The trouble with sleep, thought Emily, *is that you can't make it come when you want it.*

She lay on her back in the cupboard, in the glow of Josie's star. What *had* she seen in the forest? She'd told Dad about it when they got home, but he said it was just her imagination and there was no way he was getting the car out again in this weather.

She heard something. It was coming from the wall again – the one that separated Badger Cottage from Rufus's house. She stiffened, ready to call for Dad. But this time it wasn't that eerie wailing sound; it was more like ... well, like someone *crying*.

Being careful not to make a noise, she wriggled to the end of the cupboard and pressed her ear to the wall. Yes, definitely someone crying – a jerky sob followed by someone blowing their nose. Did Rufus have a visitor? Or another daughter?

After a few moments, it stopped. Emily sat back on her heels. She would ask Rufus next time she saw him. After all, he *had* invited her to go round and see Jacky. Whoever it was, they sounded sad, and Emily knew what *that* felt like.

She lay down again, closed her eyes and tried to picture the forest, to remember exactly how things had looked. There had been the shape on the ground – a sort of low mound. And the second shape, the one moving around – well, surely that was a lynx kitten?

A rush of sympathy washed over her. That little kitten might be out there, in the dark, on this freezing night, sniffing around its mother, who wouldn't wake up.

Hot tears needled Emily's eyes. Her hand clenched around the star as she pictured the poor little thing, whimpering and nuzzling its mother.

And she knew what she had to do.

Her stomach swooped, the way it did when she sensed the faceless monster. *No. I can't do that.* She lay completely still, her blood whooshing in her ears. *I can't. Not on my own.*

But she knew she had to.

Slowly, she slid open the cupboard door. It rattled,

and she froze. Across the landing, Dad stirred and murmured something in his sleep, but he didn't wake.

By the time Emily had pulled some warm layers over the top of her pyjamas and crept down the stairs, she was shaking so much she could hardly push her arms into the sleeves of her jacket. Her teeth chattered, even though the living room was still warm from the dying fire.

She could still go back to bed. Forget about it. She had probably imagined it.

But what if she hadn't?

Emily opened the front door and stepped out into the snowy night.

She took a deep breath and whispered to herself:

'*I'm not scared of the silly old dark,*
I'm safe and it can't hurt me.
One small light will scare it away,
So darkness, leave me be!'

It was a song that Mum used to sing to her when she was little and afraid.

Luckily the moon was out tonight, bright enough to cast shadows. But it was harder work than she had expected, trudging through the snow. There had been a fresh fall and it was halfway up her calves, covering the tyre tracks from earlier. The scrunch of the snow beneath her feet and her own panting filled her ears. She stopped every ten steps or so to listen intently, turning in a circle, checking to make sure that nothing was stalking her.

Every now and then, a heap of snow slid off a branch with a *whump* and a rustle, making her heart beat like a bird trapped inside her chest. She began to sweat inside the jacket, and unzipped it. She didn't dare think about what Dad would do if he woke up and found her gone. Shout? Definitely. Stop her going to the farm? Yes, that too. Send her away because he'd had enough of her?

Emily stopped. What if he did send her away? Where would she live? Nana Godwin didn't have room in her tiny flat. There was always Grandma Underwood, but she lived in a house full of knick-knacks and ornaments that had to be dusted every day and put back down in *exactly* the same place. She went round inspecting everything with scrunched-up lips that looked like she was sucking through an invisible straw. She even looked at Emily that way sometimes.

And if Emily went away, who would look after Dad?

She hopped up and down. What should she do? She turned around and began to tramp back through the snow, stepping in her own footprints. If she hurried, she could get back before he noticed.

But then she heard it. A strange noise coming out of the forest. Like a person grumbling and wailing without words. It reminded Emily of the noise Nana Godwin's cat made when it found a mouse, only more growly.

She stopped. Her chest felt tight and she couldn't get enough air to take a really deep breath. Should she run?

Forcing herself to move, one step at a time, she turned towards the sound and made herself walk towards the forest. It was impossible to tell where the edge of the road was, and she didn't want to sink into the ditch. She found a stick and poked it into the snow ahead of her, making sure it was safe. It was only about ten metres into the forest, no further than the width of the swimming pool back home, but it felt like ten miles.

Now she could see where the lynx lay, unmoving. It was just as she remembered it, only a bit smaller. What if it wasn't dead? What if it was just asleep, and it leapt up and sank its jaws into her throat? A little whimper escaped her.

A smaller shape skittered away into the yawning blackness between the trees.

The kitten; it had to be. But where had it gone? It may be small, but even a normal pet cat could rip your skin to shreds. She'd seen it happen to Dad, blood all over his white vet's coat.

Swallowing the lump of fear in her throat, she shuffled closer through the snow to the motionless lynx. Was it breathing? It was hard to tell, with her own breaths so hard and loud in the stillness. She forced herself to focus, to watch closely for the rise and fall of its ribs.

Nothing. Not a whisper of breath, not a twitch of a whisker.

The lynx was dead.

'Oh.' Emily gasped and pressed her hand to her lips.

She crouched by the lynx and pulled off her glove. Her hand was trembling as she laid it gently on the lynx's richly patterned coat. It was cold. Stiff. Emily bowed her head as she ran her fingers through its fur.

The scarlet bloodstain had darkened to a deep rust, and it was coming from the lynx's shoulder. Someone must have shot it. But how could that happen when the guns were all aimed upwards, at the flying pheasants?

Unless…

She got to her feet as a strange, cold feeling trickled across her skin.

Unless someone had done it on purpose.

Something in the snow caught her eye. She picked it up, turning it over and over in her hand, a hot anger seeping through her veins.

It was a red cylinder. A gun cartridge. Just like the ones in Granger's car, spilling across the back seat, next to the dead pheasants. Only this one was empty.

10

Something moved in the trees. Emily's head jerked up and she heard that same low, moaning growl. The lynx kitten hadn't gone far away.

She stepped back, away from the body, stuffing the empty cartridge into her pocket. Back she went, and back. Then she waited.

The kitten came slinking out of the trees, head hunched low into its shoulders, peering around this way and that, just as Emily had on the road. Its tufted ears flickered in every direction, though its eyes were fixed only on the lifeless shape of its mother. The streaks and spots on its coat stood out against the snow, and she saw that its stubby tail was edged with black. It looked as though the kitten had rubbed up against some dark paint, splattering it all over its beautiful golden fur.

The kitten dug its face against the mother's belly, as

though it was still trying to suck milk from her. It butted her with its head and dug its paws in, then gave up and went to her head, where it nudged her and tried to make her wake up. The desperate yowling started up again.

Yes, thought Emily, *yes, that's how I sometimes feel too.* She wanted to scoop the cub into her arms and tell it that it wasn't alone.

She knew what she had to do. Someone had to take care of that poor little lynx, and it had to be someone who knew how it felt. Dad wouldn't like it if he found out, but what was it that Mum used to say? *Sometimes it's more important to do the right thing than the easy thing.*

Emily backed away further and further until her left foot went through the snow and into the ditch beneath. Icy water filled her boot but she barely felt it. *Slosh, squelch,* it went as she walked back down the lane to the cottage.

What if the lynx kitten went off on its own while she was away? She broke into a run. And what if the person who had shot the mother came back and killed the kitten? She ran faster. Twice, she slipped and fell on her hands and knees in the ever-deepening snow. Twice, she struggled to her feet and kept on going.

The cottage windows were dark when she got back. Good. That meant Dad was still asleep. The back door creaked as she let herself into the kitchen. There must be some meat in the fridge. She found a tray of minced beef, blood pooling in the bottom where it had defrosted.

Tiredness began to drag at her hands and feet. It was such an effort to think about going out into the cold. Should she go upstairs and find some dry socks? It was very tempting – she could just lie down for a few minutes to warm up and have a rest...

Wake up, Emily! She shook her head like a dog coming out of a river and opened the door.

The walk back along the lane to the ditch seemed three times further than it had before. Surely she must have gone past it? Once she even went back to look, thinking she might have dozed off and actually sleepwalked past the spot. But no, she could still see the dark shapes of the cottage and Rufus's taller house beside it. She'd hardly got anywhere.

Blinking with exhaustion, she staggered on through the snow, clutching the mince in its plastic container. Thoughts whispered at the back of her mind. *Go back. Don't be so silly, Emily. What do you think you're doing?* Some of them were in Emily's own voice, and some of them were in Dad's.

But she was used to not listening to those, so she blocked them out and walked on.

Her own footprints led her back at last to the ditch, where a dark slash of mud and melted snow marked the right spot.

A movement in the trees caught her eye. The lynx kitten was still there, darting at its mother and nipping her – on her face, her paws, her flanks. Nipping and biting to try and get her to stand up.

All of a sudden, Emily's plan seemed like the most stupid thing in the whole world. But now she was here, she didn't know what else to do. She tore open the plastic cover on the minced beef package as quietly as she could. Digging her fingers into the red worms of meat, she broke off a chunk and threw it towards the kitten. It must be starving by now, without its mother to help it find food.

The meat lay on the snow.

Emily waited.

Nothing happened.

A slow disappointment crept over her, beginning in her stomach and tightening her chest and throat. Stupid, stupid idea. Why did nothing ever go right any more? The lump in her throat grew into a ball of tears and she couldn't shift it no matter how hard she swallowed. She squeezed her eyes shut, to hold the tears in. What was she *doing*, standing here in the snow, in the dark?

This was it. This was when the faceless monster would find her, all alone in the cold starlight. She could feel its presence, creeping nearer, waiting to smother her, to suffocate the life out of her.

She wanted to make a noise like the lynx kitten. Just to see if anyone out there was listening. Maybe if she howled loud enough, Mum would hear it wherever she was.

A slight shuffling sound in the snow. Emily opened her eyes.

The kitten was eating the meat.

'Good girl,' whispered Emily, although the lynx could be a boy for all she knew. 'How about a little more?' She stepped back on to the lane and dropped another chunk of meat, red against the snow.

When it came, stepping and sniffing, she almost squeaked with excitement.

The lynx licked up the fallen mince and looked up, straight at Emily. She dropped another piece, and the lynx crept closer. Back and back Emily went, leaving her meaty trail in the snow. Little by little, on came the lynx.

Emily forgot about the cold. She forgot all about her own fear. She just wanted to bring the lynx safely home. It was only when she reached the gateway to the courtyard that she realised: where could she put it? She couldn't take it indoors. For one thing, Dad would blow his top and take the lynx away. For another, it would be frightened with all the lights and noises of the house. It was used to the dark peace of the forest.

Dark.

Of course. The old outside toilet. It was dark and safe, and without a window there was no chance of anyone looking in and finding it by accident.

Emily eased the gate open and made sure the lynx could see her disappearing into the courtyard. There was hardly any meat left now, only a piece the size of a golf ball. She broke it into three tiny pieces and left the first one in the gateway. The second she placed halfway between the gate and the outhouse, and the third she put right inside. It was invisible in the blackness, but surely the lynx would be able to smell it?

Hardly able to breathe, she hid in the shadows and watched. Here it came – step, sniff, step, sniff … stop. Step, sniff again.

It stopped right outside the outhouse. *Go in*, urged Emily silently.

Suddenly, the courtyard was flooded with light

from the cottage. Dad's bedroom light was on. He would know that she'd gone out.

Emily leapt out of the shadows. The lynx peeled back its lips in a terrified snarl. It arched its back and made a strange hiss-growl.

'Go *in*.' Emily stamped on the ground and the lynx backed away, into the outhouse. Emily pushed the door firmly shut. There was a hook on the outside, which fitted into a loop of metal. She dropped the hook into the loop just as the kitchen light came on, the back door slammed back and Dad stormed out.

11

At breakfast the next morning, Dad wouldn't speak. He was so angry that the skin under his eye kept twitching.

Emily didn't care. She preferred him quiet to when he was yelling at her, like he had last night. She had told him that she hadn't been able to sleep, so she had gone outside to play in the snow. It wasn't a very good lie, but he had seemed to believe her. He had shouted at her until the lights had gone on in Rufus's house, too. Then he had gone quietly furious and dragged her indoors by the elbow. If she went deaf, it would be all his fault.

She thought about the massive problem she now had.

Number one, she wasn't allowed out of Dad's sight today. Even when she went upstairs to the toilet, he hovered outside the door, the floorboards creaking under his feet.

Number two, the lynx was shut in the outhouse with no light and no food and not even a blanket to keep it warm. Somehow, Emily *had* to find a way to slip outside, even for a few minutes.

Dad's phone rang, just as he was putting a couple of slices of bread into the toaster. He peered at the screen.

'Surgery. Why do they keep ringing me? I'm not even working for them yet.'

His face was still crumpled in the same scowl that he'd woken up with. As she chewed her breakfast cereal, Emily thought about the photograph he'd brought from home, the one that stood on his bedside table in a silver frame. It was a picture of him and Mum on their wedding day. His hair had been black as the night sky then, without the grey sprinkles, and his whole face had been one huge smile as he looked at Mum adoringly. Mum used to pick that photo up and tell Emily that he had worn that same smile the first time he had cradled her in his arms as a newborn baby. She searched his face now to see if there were traces of it hidden beneath his skin.

'Hello? Matt speaking. A what? When? You're *kidding*.' He sighed heavily. 'Yes, I'll come and give you a hand.' He slammed the phone down on to the table, next to the *'No Lynx in Littendale'* leaflet.

Emily paused, cereal spoon halfway to her mouth. 'What?'

'One of the lynx has been killed. Shot, they think. But worse still, the stupid...' He swallowed a swear word and his Adam's apple bulged with the effort. 'The *idiots* have taken the kitten.'

Emily put the spoon down. She wasn't hungry.

'Perhaps they're looking after it,' she said, cringing away from Dad as he stamped around the kitchen.

'Looking after it?' he spat. 'You have to know what you're doing to look after a wild animal. It's not a tame kitten. Plus it's a criminal offence to hold a wild animal without a proper licence.'

Emily swallowed. 'Criminal?'

Dad didn't seem to hear her. 'And the surgery's short-staffed today so they've asked if I'll go and take a look at the carcass to confirm the cause of death. It's not something I want you to see, so what am I supposed to do with you?' He ran his hands through his hair so that it stood up in angry tufts. 'I want you where I can see you today.'

The smell of burning toast filled the kitchen and the smoke alarm shrieked.

'For crying out loud!' Dad stood on his chair and ripped the entire smoke alarm off the ceiling.

Silence fell.

Emily gulped. 'What if there's a fire?'

'Then we'll all die in our beds!'

The toast popped, making them both jump. Dad pulled out the two blackened pieces, yanked open the back door and hurled them into the yard. Emily could see the door of the outhouse and wondered what was going on inside. The lynx would need food and water. Perhaps it would like some milk, too.

'Josie can watch me,' she suggested, although she hated the thought. She didn't really want to see Josie again, but maybe Josie would get so caught up with her painting that she wouldn't notice if Emily were to sneak off...

Dad puffed out his cheeks and let out a long breath, like a balloon going down. He rested his hands on the kitchen bench and bowed his head.

'I don't like to ask her again,' he said at last, 'but you're right; it's probably the best idea.'

Emily looked down into her bowl of soggy chocolate hoops. She hoped Josie wouldn't want to ask her about Mum and go on about what happened last time with the star and everything.

'But if I ever catch the person who's got that lynx kitten,' Dad went on, winding himself up again, 'I'll personally stuff them, roast them slowly over a hot fire and serve them up for Christmas dinner.'

Emily swallowed, feeling the heat of that fire spreading from her chest right through her whole body.

☙

The welcome owl had been put back on its perch, but Emily was pleased to see that it had a big crack across its head. *Serves it right for being so smug*, she thought, flicking it with her finger as she went past.

Dad didn't knock. 'Josie?' he called as he opened the door. 'Are you in here?'

Josie's surprised face appeared round the sliding door, a mug in her hand. She was wearing glasses today.

'Just having a camomile tea to start the day on a *calm* note.' She looked at Dad over the top of her glasses. 'Would you care for one?'

'Thank you, but no,' he said. 'I have to go out. I know it's a lot to ask, but could you possibly watch Emily for a while?'

'Well, I suppose… How does Emily feel about it?'

Emily opened her mouth to say that she was perfectly fine on her own – after all, she would be going to secondary school next year, and nobody needed a babysitter at her age – but Dad beat her to it.

'It doesn't matter how Emily feels,' he said. 'I'm afraid her behaviour means that right now I can't trust her to be left alone. Not today.'

Josie raised her eyebrows at Emily. 'Goodness, what on earth have you been doing?'

A rising tide of worry swirled around her chest. She had to get to the lynx. What if it starved to death? She'd left it in the dark on its own and it would think that nobody cared. Plus it might start making that growly miaowing noise.

'I don't mind staying with Josie,' she said, 'if Josie doesn't mind.'

'Of course I don't.' Josie smiled as though the whole silly business with the star had never happened.

Dad looked at Emily wearily. 'This is your last chance, Em. If this isn't going to work for us, I'll drive you to Grandma Underwood's and you can stay with her for the next six months.'

The worry threatened to spill over, and Emily had to take several deep breaths to keep it in. This was all going so *wrong* already. If Dad – or anyone else – discovered the lynx in the outhouse...

It didn't bear thinking about.

12

'I'm really sorry about the other day,' said Josie. 'I had no idea. The last thing I intended was to upset you.'

Emily knew she probably should apologise as well, for storming off. But she didn't *feel* sorry, so it would be stupid to say that she was. She picked up a fir cone encrusted with glitter and picked off a blob of transparent glue.

'Thank you for the star,' she said stiffly.

'You're welcome,' said Josie. 'I'm going to finish painting. Do you want to have a go too? I can give you a brush and some paints.'

Emily shook her head. 'Do you mind if I play out in the courtyard?'

'Your dad said I mustn't let you out of my sight.'

Emily picked up a green glass bottle and blew across the top of it, making a low hooting sound. 'I'd rather play in the snow. We never get snow like this back home.'

'It *is* rather magical, isn't it? How about I come out and help you build a snowman?'

She guessed that Josie's snowman would be perfectly shaped, with all its features carefully carved and its hair made of moss. Not like the fat blobs that Emily and Mum used to make, giggling together as they pinched Dad's best scarf and fastened it round the snowman's neck.

'No thanks. I want to make a den in the outhouse.'

'Not scared of spiders?'

'No way.'

Josie puffed out her cheeks. 'I suppose it wouldn't do any harm…'

'You can see me if you just step outside the door and I promise-promise-*promise* not to go out of the gate. I'll be in the cottage or in my den.'

'All right.' Josie pushed her glasses up to the top of her head, where they sat like a second pair of eyes. 'But promise that if I call you, you'll come straight away. Don't want to get into trouble with your dad, do we?'

She turned back to her canvas, humming a Christmas carol under her breath.

Emily turned, knocking against a table. Something fell out of her pocket. The gun cartridge.

Josie scooped it up and handed it back. 'Where did you find that? One of Rufus's old ones, no doubt, although I've only ever seen him with the blue ones.'

'What's the difference?' asked Emily.

Josie shrugged. 'I'm not really sure. Different size, maybe? Or different make? I expect he has all kinds. That man will shoot anything. It should be against the law.'

Emily's fingers closed around the gun cartridge. Of course. Rufus had a gun too, didn't he? And he hated the whole Lynx Link business. Maybe it wasn't Granger who shot the kitten's mother.

She raced outside and pressed her ear to the door of the outhouse. She listened as hard as she could, but she couldn't hear a thing. Perhaps the lynx was asleep. Or what if it had died in the night? It had looked healthy enough, but she hadn't fed it since last night, and what if...?

Her hand was on the latch, ready to pull the door open, but she stopped herself. Kitchen first. She would get some food and water and a blanket, and then come back and open the door. Yes, that was definitely the right thing to do.

There were a couple of sausages in the fridge, left over from last night's supper. Emily nibbled the end of one. It tasted even better than it had last night, and if she dipped it in some tomato ketchup – just a little squeeze – it would be even nicer.

A minute later there was only one sausage. Emily looked at it, the taste of guilt filling her mouth. One sausage wasn't enough. There must be something else.

After rummaging around in the freezer, she found some steak and popped it into the microwave to defrost while she went upstairs. There was a spare blanket folded neatly on a shelf in the top of Dad's wardrobe, so she dragged that out and took it downstairs. She filled a plastic ice cream tub with milk and then sat down at the table with all the uncleared breakfast things, mashing the remains of her cereal with the back of a spoon while she waited for the microwave to ping.

When she had everything ready, she left it all piled on the kitchen bench and darted across the snowy courtyard to Josie's studio.

'Just checking in,' she said, as she poked her head round the door. 'Letting you know I'm still here.'

'Thanks,' called Josie. 'If you do that every few minutes, I'll know everything's okay.'

Emily ducked back outside, scooped up a handful of snow and smashed it on to the welcome owl's head. Then she scurried back to the kitchen, grabbed the tub, meat and blanket, and went to the outhouse. Taking a deep breath, she braced herself, ready to stop the lynx if it tried to dart past her and escape.

The first thing to hit her when she opened the door was the smell. The lynx had done a shedload of poo in the night. As the wintry light flooded in, it leapt up and pressed itself against the back wall, hissing and spitting.

Emily pulled the door closed behind her, leaving the tiniest gap to let light in. She hoped the lynx wouldn't try and get past her. 'Shhh, it's all right,' she crooned. 'I won't hurt you. Look, I brought you some milk.'

She crouched to put the ice cream tub on the ground. The lynx sprang forward and raked its claws into the back of her hand. It hurt worse than the time at school when she stapled her finger with the teacher's staple gun, but she pressed the blanket to it and gritted her teeth.

The lynx was against the back wall again, its eyes fixed on her face. *Don't stare at it*, she thought, remembering the advice Dad had given her for dealing with a cat at the surgery. If you stared into a cat's eyes, it would feel threatened and attack you.

Still murmuring to the lynx, Emily laid out the blanket on a cleanish patch of floor. The closer she was to the ground, the more it stank, and she had to breathe through her mouth to shut out the smell. She would have to find something to clean up the poo with – a spade or something.

She put the sausage down, as close to the lynx as she could, but ready to leap back out of the way of its claws.

'Come and try this,' she said. 'It's good, I promise you.' Perhaps she should have heated it up so the lynx could smell it. Lying there like that, the sausage looked like some kind of giant slug. The steak, then. Raw meat was what the lynx would eat in the wild.

She carefully laid out three slices of steak. Dad was bound to notice they were gone. She would have to find a way of replacing them from her pocket money. But she didn't get that much, and how was she supposed to slip off to the butcher's if he wouldn't let her go off on her own?

Suddenly it all seemed too much – the days ahead of skulking about, stealing food, trying to replace it, trying not to get caught. And the lynx wasn't eating any of it. She had wanted to take care of it, and all she had done was scare it even more.

As she toppled backwards and sat, she allowed herself a single sob. Just one. It wouldn't change anything. That was one thing she'd learnt over the last six months – crying changed nothing.

She hooked her arms around her knees and rested her head there, eyes closed. She was just so *tired*. And she would have to get up in a couple of minutes to go inside so Josie didn't come to check on her.

She realised that the spitting and growling had stopped. Moving only the tiniest muscle at a time, she raised her head ever so slightly.

The lynx, pressing itself flat against the floor, was creeping out of its corner. Its ears swivelled in every direction and it eyes constantly flickered between Emily and the steak.

Don't move, Emily willed herself, even though an itch had started in her nose and a cough was building in her throat.

Paw by stealthy paw, the lynx moved towards the steak. When it was near enough, its front paw flashed out. It hooked one slice of meat with a claw and skittered back into the spider-infested corner. It watched her warily as it wolfed down the meat.

'Good girl,' said Emily, her lips barely moving. The kitten's fur was so pretty up close, with all the dark spots and smudges scattered across the gold. Its eyes were outlined in black, as though it had make-up on. 'Good girl, Lotta. Lotta Spots, that can be your name.'

Watching Lotta eat, Emily could hardly bear to tear herself away, but she still had the poo to clean up.

And Josie to keep an eye on. This wasn't going to be easy.

'Stay here,' she whispered. Lotta looked up at her, still chewing the steak. 'I'll be back soon.'

After a quick peek into the studio, a shout to Josie and another heap of snow on the welcome owl, Emily looked around for something to clean up with. It was easy enough to find an old plastic bag in a kitchen drawer, but she needed a spade, like the plastic beach ones from the summer holidays. Not that they'd gone anywhere last summer.

She dug deep into the back of each drawer until she found a giant spoon with holes in it, which Dad used for draining pasta. That would be a perfect poo scoop, and if he needed it, she could make some excuse.

When Emily eased open the door of the outhouse, she was thrilled to see the second slice of steak had vanished and Lotta was licking her paws. The instant she saw Emily, though, she leapt to her feet, bristling all over like a toilet brush.

'Easy, Lotta. Just going to … pick up this … eerrggh…' Emily gagged as she scooped up the poo and tipped it into the plastic bag. But at last it was done. She really couldn't stay here, because Dad could be back any minute. 'I'll come back when I can,' she whispered. 'Don't worry about your mum. I'm here to take care of you.'

Just in time. Dad came stomping down the lane and into the courtyard.

'I thought Josie was keeping an eye on you,' he said.

'I am,' trilled Josie, stepping out at just the right moment, as though she'd been watching out of the window the whole time. 'She's been good as gold. Not set foot outside the gate once.'

'Hmm.' Dad folded his arms. 'What's in the bag?' He nodded at the plastic bag hooked over Emily's arm, which smelled pretty gross.

'Just some … er … dog muck that was in the yard. I picked it up.'

'Disgusting,' said Josie, pulling a face. 'People shouldn't be allowed to own dogs if they let them do that sort of thing.'

Dad ruffled Emily's hair, his face relaxing into something more like a smile. 'Good for you. Fancy coming into the village? I need to get some potatoes. Thought I'd have a go at making some chips.'

Emily bounced up and down, the bag swinging against her leg, forgetting her troubles for a moment. 'Goody! What will we have them with?'

Dad smiled properly this time. 'I've got a tasty bit of steak in the freezer. We'll have that.'

13

For the first time in her life, Emily wasn't enjoying the snow. Normally she'd be jumping and hopping as she walked along, trailing her hand along the walls to scoop up great armfuls. Today she was too busy worrying. How come she always had such bad luck? That steak had been in the freezer all week and Dad hadn't mentioned it. Now she would have to replace it at once, but she only had ninety pence in her purse.

'Where will we get the potatoes?' she asked, keeping her head down and watching the green tips of her wellington boots flash in and out of her vision. *Right, left; right, left.*

'Butcher has some. I'll pick up some bacon at the same time.'

Great. So she couldn't even slip into the butcher's on her own. Emily felt as though a hand was squeezing her throat, making it difficult to breathe.

'Can I buy something in the village?' she asked. *Right, left.*

'Why? If you need something, I'll get it for you.' Dad's shoulders were hunched, his hands deep in his pockets.

Emily thought quickly. 'It's for a Christmas present.' She hated lying, but Dad could never tell. Not like Mum, who had sniffed out a lie the moment it entered Emily's head, before she even spoke it. 'And can I have my pocket money? Otherwise I won't have enough money to buy it.' *Right, left.*

'Ah, in that case…' Dad brought out his wallet and pulled out a five-pound note. 'Is that enough? I don't know what you'll find in Littendale, though. Is it for Nana Godwin?'

Emily shrugged. 'Not exactly.'

Dad tapped the side of his nose. 'Say no more.'

Emily's heart sank. Now he thought that she was buying a present for *him,* which meant that she would have to find more money from somewhere to get that as well. *Right, left; right, left.*

'Hey, Soup!' It was Dibs, bounding up behind them, scraping up snow from the wall with his hand. 'Where you off to?'

Emily dropped back. Dad went ahead while she fell into step with Dibs. 'Shopping,' she said.

Dibs snorted. 'Good luck with that. Not much to buy in Littendale. Alexander says hi, by the way.' She couldn't think who Dibs was talking about. 'Well, strictly speaking he didn't say hi, he said *miaoooow*.'

'Where are you going?' she asked. 'Shouldn't you be at the farm?'

But Dibs was already running ahead, his long legs stretching over the snow. He reminded her of a hare.

'Tell you later,' he called over his shoulder. 'Or tomorrow. Come and see Alexander.'

It took about ten minutes to get to the heart of the village, where the butcher's shop was squeezed next to the post office and general village store. Neither of them had any customers. The butcher was standing outside, sleeves rolled up to reveal huge, meaty forearms. He was staring a little way down the road, frowning and shaking his head.

Emily looked too. Gathered in front of a small terraced house was a crowd of people, shouting and holding up big signs on sticks. Emily had seen stuff like this on the evening news.

'Is it a protest?' she said, as she caught up with Dad.

His scowl had returned and he didn't answer the question. Instead, he motioned to her to stand aside. 'Wait here. Keep out of the way.'

Normally, Emily would have put on her own protest at that, but she realised that this was her golden opportunity to buy the meat.

'I'll get the potatoes,' she called.

Dad was already walking away, towards the protest.

'Excuse me,' said Emily to the butcher. 'Can I buy something from your shop?'

The butcher cleared his throat. Close up, he looked a bit piggy, with his small eyes and a nose that turned up at the end.

'Of course. Come inside. Seen enough of that lot anyway.' He led the way into the shop, which was very cold and smelled strange – it reminded Emily of the time she had a massive nose bleed into the kitchen sink and Mum had cleaned it out with disinfectant. 'Now what can I get you, little lady?'

Emily clutched the five-pound note tightly in her fist and stared at all the cuts of meat laid out under the glass. Fat fillets of chicken, slabs of pork, a long string of sausages heaped up on top of itself. What would Lotta like best? In the corner was some dark meat – *venison* said the label. That was deer meat, wasn't it? Just like Lotta would eat in the wild. But she had to get the steak first, so that Dad wouldn't suspect anything.

'First of all, I would like three pieces of steak if you've got any.' One for her, one for Dad and one for

Lotta. It had taken ages for Dad to stop cooking enough food for three; the bin was always full of wasted pasta or curry that he couldn't bring himself to eat when he'd really made it for Mum.

The butcher slapped some meat on to a piece of greaseproof paper and weighed it on some scales. Then he wrapped it up and put a sticker on the paper to hold it closed, and slipped it all into a small plastic bag. 'Anything else?'

'Some venison, please. A medium-sized piece.'

The butcher weighed out the venison and slapped a second bag on to the counter. 'That it?'

Emily curled and uncurled the five-pound note. 'How much have I already spent?'

The butcher did a quick calculation in his head. 'Eleven pounds eighty-seven.'

'*Eleven pounds…*'

The butcher nodded. 'And eighty-seven pence.'

'I don't have enough,' said Emily in a small voice. 'How much is just the steak?'

'Seven twenty. It's top quality.'

'I still don't have enough.'

The butcher sighed. 'Tell you what, I'll take out one of the slices of steak and the venison and we'll call it evens.'

He fiddled about with the package and handed it

to Emily, who gave him the five-pound note and waited hopefully for the change that never came.

'Thank you,' she remembered to say as she walked slowly out of the shop. Now what? She had replaced the steak, but she had nothing new to give to Lotta, and now she had to get a Christmas present as well, and she'd already had her pocket money and … and she'd still forgotten to buy the potatoes.

The crowd roared. A door opened in the house they were standing outside. People shifted enough for Emily to see the notice in the window: *LYNX LINK PROJECT, REGIONAL OFFICE.*

'Calm down, folks, calm down.' A man came out, cramming a bobble hat on to his head. The bobble jiggled every time he spoke.

Andy. From the forest. Emily hid the bag of steak under her coat and went closer.

'Let's talk about this in a civilised manner,' said Andy. 'If I have to call the police, I will.'

Another angry cry went up, and people waved their placards: *No Lynx in Littendale. Lynx Stinks. Save Our Stock.*

Emily spotted Granger, leaning against the low stone wall across the road, lighting a cigarette. His eyes slid towards her and she leapt back, as though he could see everything she was hiding.

'I know you're hiding something too,' she muttered, thinking of the red shotgun cartridge stuffed inside an odd sock in her drawer. 'And I'm going to make sure everyone knows it.'

'We're just protecting our livestock,' someone shouted out. 'We don't need the lynx in Littendale.'

'But you do.' Dad's voice rang out over the crowd. 'They're a good thing for this village. That forest is getting overrun with deer, which get out and damage growing crops and trees. The lynx will keep the deer population down and return the ecosystem to its natural balance, not to mention…'

His voice was drowned in a roar of protest, and Emily noticed with a sinking heart that Rufus Hardacre stood at the edge of the group, arms folded across his chest. Almost as though he sensed her watching, he turned and frowned. He began to amble towards her, leaning heavily on some kind of pointy stick. Jacky trotted at his heels, head high, sniffing the air.

'Good afternoon, young lady, hmm?' said Rufus.

Emily wasn't sure whether she was supposed to answer. Was he asking her whether she was having a good afternoon (to which the answer was most definitely *no*) or was he just saying hello? She didn't have long to decide, because he kept on talking.

'I suggest that you persuade your father to keep his opinions to himself in a small village like this one. He's not going to be popular, hmm?'

Jacky jumped up against Emily's leg. The steak was cold and clammy beneath her coat, and the package suddenly dropped out, on to the toe of her wellington boot. Jacky barked and tried to tear it open.

'Away, Jacky,' snapped Rufus, sweeping the little dog aside with his stick. He regarded the package for a long moment before looking up at her, his eyes bloodshot. 'If I see one of those feral cats anywhere near my property, I'll shoot it. *BANG*.'

Emily jumped, and the steak fell off her foot into the snow.

'Better pick that up, hmm?' said Rufus. 'Before it comes to any harm.' He turned his back on her and ambled away, back towards the crowd.

14

'That's odd,' said Dad, rummaging in the freezer. 'This steak is half defrosted. Did you leave the freezer open today?'

'No.' Emily pretended to be busy setting the table.

'And I could have sworn there were three pieces.' He shook his head and gave a dry little laugh. 'Must be going mad in my old age.'

He rattled about with a frying pan and soon the smell of sizzling steak filled the kitchen. Emily flitted about the room, picking things up and putting them down again.

'Stop fidgeting and do something useful,' said Dad. 'Since we both forgot the potatoes, we'll have to have pasta instead. Okay with you?'

Emily nodded. She was desperate to get outside and check on Lotta, but Dad had kept her close by him all afternoon.

'So, did you get me a good present?' Dad uncorked a bottle of red wine and poured himself a glass.

'No-o. Not exactly.'

He laughed. 'Don't worry, you don't have to tell me. Keep your secret.'

Emily felt a bit sick. She was beginning to wish she'd never got into this secret in the first place.

'Now, where's that spoon for draining the pasta?'

Emily swallowed. Was this her chance?

'It's – um – outside.'

'Outside?'

'I was using it to … play in the snow.'

Dad took another swig of wine. 'Go and get it, then. I need it.'

Her wellies stood where she'd left them when she got back from the village, racing ahead of Dad to get the steak in the freezer before he noticed. They were cold when she pushed her feet into them and, scrunching up her toes as tightly as she could, she stepped out into the bitter evening.

Thankfully, the kitchen window was completely steamed up so Dad wouldn't be able to see what she was doing, even if he did look out. Emily hurried to the outhouse and opened the door. Lotta Spots did her usual thing of pressing herself into the corner and hissing.

'Oh, Lotta. I'm just trying to help you. Please don't be mad at me.' She had to cup her hand to her mouth to try and catch the sob that was waiting to jump out. 'And you haven't even had any milk.'

The plastic container had been knocked over, and there was milk all over the floor.

Emily looked at the door. It would be so easy to just leave it open and let Lotta go. But would she be able to survive on her own? What if she went on to the road and got run over? Or went back to the forest to look for her mother, who wasn't even there any more? She might not be able to hunt for her own food yet. What if Rufus saw her? Or Granger? They would probably shoot her.

Whatever Emily did, it was almost certain to go horribly wrong. She needed to tell someone – someone who would know what to do.

Of course.

There was someone.

Remembering at last what she had come for, Emily picked up the giant poo-collecting spoon from the floor and dried her tears on her sleeve. Whispering a last goodnight, she stepped outside and pulled the door shut. She dug about in the snow with the spoon, knowing she'd need to wash it properly before Dad used it to drain the pasta.

Picking up two handfuls of snow, she rubbed it all over her cheeks. Let him tell her off for messing about and getting wet; at least he wouldn't know she'd been crying.

'Dibs, I've got something to tell you. I need your help.' He was in the old shed the next morning, kneeling over something. Streak was nearby, digging, as usual, in the red-speckled earth beneath the old tractor. 'What are you doing?'

Dibs straightened up, a can of spray paint in his hand. 'What do you think of that?'

Emily sucked in her breath. Dibs had sprayed in bright blue paint on a huge piece of board: *Big Cats Mean Big Troble*.

'It's spelt wrong,' she managed to say.

Dibs cursed under his breath and added a 'u' to make 'trouble'. 'Now it looks a right mess. I'll have to start again.' He shoved the board against the wall and took another one.

'Were you at that protest yesterday?' Her mouth felt all dry and her voice came out a bit squeaky, but Dibs didn't seem to notice. He was already spraying the new board with the same message, spelt correctly

103

this time. The smell of the paint filled the shed, making Emily's head swim.

'Yeah, did you see it?' Dibs pushed his hair out of his eyes with his forearm and painted a fat paw print at the bottom of the sheet. 'There's another one this afternoon, but this time we're going to the County Council. Off to the big boys!'

'So, you're against the Lynx Link too?'

Dibs put the lid on the spray paint can and sat back, kneeling in the dirt. 'Big cats, small lambs. Predators and prey. They don't belong together, do they, Soup? It's obvious. And one of them was here again, the other day. We saw the print.'

'But they won't do any harm. They...'

Dibs pulled a face. 'So you know all about it, do you,' he said, 'coming from a town and all?'

'Just because I lived in a town...'

'Bet you think that lambs are all cute and fluffy and shouldn't end up on people's plates.'

'Well...' She *did* think that, and so what? Plus she didn't actually eat lamb, which meant that *she* would never be responsible for...

'You do. I knew it.' Dibs hooted and clapped his hands. 'Caught you out there, Soup.' He looked proudly at his sign again. 'So, what is it, then?'

'What?'

'What did you want to tell me? You need help with something.'

Nessie and Bean came racing in from the yard. Still no school, then. Or maybe they'd broken up for the holidays.

'Oh, it's you again,' said Nessie. 'Have you come to see your kitten?'

Bean crouched beside Dibs and picked up the paint can; Dibs snatched it away from him.

'Alexander's not *my* kitten,' said Emily, although she wished he was. Mind you, she had enough on her plate coping with Lotta. Alexander was better off here, with a family to take care of him.

'Are you Dibs's girlfriend?' sniggered Nessie.

'Of course I'm not,' said Emily, blushing.

'Course she's not,' echoed Dibs. 'She's my friend and she came to tell me something. Didn't you?'

It was Emily's turn to scowl. 'It doesn't matter. You wouldn't understand, being a *lynx hater* and all.'

There was a beat of silence. Dibs stood and drew himself up to his full height, which was quite a bit taller than Emily. He stood toe to toe with her, his eyes dark with fury. 'If your dad was in hospital and there was no money coming in, and there was some wild animal out there that could come in and kill half your flock, you might have the first idea of why I hate those cats. I bet you've never had to face anything like that.'

Emily clenched her fists. Her fingers felt all fizzy and for a moment she wanted to punch Dibs really hard. He folded his arms, as if to say, *I've won this argument and you know it.*

'Actually,' she said, sounding out each syllable so it came out as *ak-chew-al-ly*, 'my mum was killed in a car crash last summer. I'm sorry about your dad and everything, but you're not the only one with problems.'

Dibs's mouth fell open. 'I ... I didn't...'

'So you don't know as much as you think you do.'

She scuffed at a pile of straw that had fallen from a bale, not knowing whether to feel angry or upset or disappointed. In fact, she felt curiously numb. If she couldn't tell Dibs about Lotta Spots, who would help her?

Nobody, that's who. She was on her own. Same as ever.

She felt that panicky feeling – the faceless monster was close by. She hadn't sensed it so much these last couple of days, since she'd found Lotta. But it was close now, ever so close.

'I have to go.'

'Wait,' said Dibs, taking her elbow. 'Don't be like

that. Come on, you said you had something to tell me. I'm listening.'

Emily shook her head. She just wanted to get home now. 'It doesn't matter. Not now.' Away she walked, faster and faster until she broke into a run at the gate, with Dibs calling after her.

'It does matter,' he yelled. 'I'm sorry, all right?'

But it was too late for sorry. There was only one person she really wanted to speak to.

And that was never going to happen again.

15

The man on the TV weather forecast was skipping about more than usual. 'It looks as though we might actually get a white Christmas,' he announced, waving his hand at the great chunks of white spread over his map of the British Isles. 'We have an amber weather warning for snow in the north, which means you can expect disruption to travel and power supplies.'

'Great,' said Dad, stifling a yawn. 'Just what we need. Hope Nana Godwin can get through.'

Emily, who was lying full length on the slouchy sofa, trying to get Wi-Fi on her tablet, sat up. 'What do you mean? She's coming on the train, you said so.'

'Easy, tiger.' Dad scratched his stubble. 'I'm sure it'll be fine. She'll be here for Christmas.'

'Can I ring her?'

Dad tossed his phone over. 'You can try, but the signal's a bit iffy. Kitchen seems to be best.'

Emily padded into the kitchen, her thick socks slipping on the tiles, and punched Nana Godwin's number into the keypad. Two little bars on the screen told her there was a signal and, sure enough, the phone began to ring. Emily waited. And waited. After a few rings, the answerphone voice cut in – a very posh lady explaining that Nana wasn't available right now, but if she'd like to leave a message…

Emily put the phone down on the table and sighed. She'd have to try again later.

Maybe this was a good chance to slip out and see Lotta? Easing the fridge door open as quietly as she could, she scanned the shelves for meat. Dad had been back to the butcher that morning and stocked up on bacon and some chopped-up chicken for a stir-fry.

'Hungry?' Dad came in. 'I'm not surprised – you didn't eat much at lunchtime. Or at tea yesterday. You gone off pasta all of a sudden?'

'I wouldn't mind a bacon sandwich,' said Emily, although she really wasn't hungry at all. But she might be able to slip the bacon to Lotta, and then she wouldn't have to replace it because Dad would think *she'd* eaten it. Sometimes her brain ached with all this roundabout thinking.

'I was saving that for brekkie,' said Dad. 'But if there's a chance of losing power, we should probably eat up the fresh stuff in case the fridge goes off. Maybe you could make a start on decorating that Christmas tree while you're waiting?' He switched on the gas and a blue flame leapt beneath the frying pan.

The tree stood in its pot. Next to it was Josie's box of decorations – all handmade, of course; all very pretty, but not the *right* decorations. Those were in the loft back at home. Decorating the tree was something that Emily and Mum had done together every year. Always with a playlist of Christmas carols on; always with a warm mince pie afterwards and sometimes a mug of creamy hot chocolate with marshmallows floating in it.

Dad peeled off four rashers of bacon and dropped them into the pan so they spat and popped. 'Well, what do you think?'

But all she could think about was Mum, handing her decorations and suggesting where they might go, but always, *always* letting Emily have the final say.

'No,' said Emily shortly. 'You do it.'

'You know I'm useless at that sort of thing.' Dad forced a laugh. 'It would probably end up looking like an explosion in a Christmas factory.' He poked at the bacon with a fork and sighed. 'Let's leave it for now, hey? There's no rush.'

Emily put her head down on the table. When she kicked her foot against the table leg, it sounded loud, like a giant's footsteps. She imagined being a giant, striding across the snowy fields to fetch Nana Godwin. Nobody would argue with Emily then, or tell her what to do. She could take all the meat she wanted from the butcher, or just pick up a whole deer out of the forest and feed it to Lotta.

The phone buzzed on the table, sending a vibration right into her head.

'Nana?' She kept her head down on the table and pressed the phone to her ear.

Nana sounded breathless, as though she'd been running. 'Matt? Is everything all right?'

'It's me – Emily.'

She could pretty much hear Nana smiling as her voice took on the warm, husky tone that she used for bedtime stories. 'Emily, my darling girl! How are you?'

Emily shot a glance towards Dad, turning the rashers of bacon over. 'I'm ... okay, I suppose.'

'That doesn't sound too good to me, pumpkin. Want to talk to me about it?'

'Yes, oh yes, I *do*, but ... I can't.'

Nana's voice seemed to get closer, as though she

had her mouth pressed right up against the phone. 'You can tell me anything. I don't mind what it is.'

'I would, Nana, but...' She let out a frustrated sigh as Dad cut in with a *'Who is it?'* from across the kitchen.

'Ah, your dad's there, right? And it's something you can't say with him standing near you?'

Emily nodded in relief. Then she realised that Nana Godwin couldn't see her. 'Yes. Yes, that's it. Exactly.'

'O-kaay. So we need to play a guessing game here. Is it something your dad's done that you're upset about?'

'No, not really.' Although he *had* upset her by shouting so much.

'Is it something *you've* done that's wrong, but you don't want to tell him?'

Emily hesitated. *Had* she done something wrong? She thought of Lotta nuzzling her dead mother in the snow. 'No, not that.'

'Is it something you need help with?'

'Yes, definitely that.'

'And can it wait until I get there in a couple of days?'

'I guess.' It couldn't, not really, but perhaps she could hang on till then. Nana Godwin would know just what to do about Lotta Spots. 'Can't you come tomorrow?'

Emily heard Nana sucking at her false teeth. 'I've booked my train ticket for Christmas Eve. I don't think I can change it now.'

'You will come, won't you? Even if it's really, really snowy?'

'I'll be there. You can count on that.'

Dad put a plate down on the table next to Emily's head. She never knew that a bacon sandwich could sound so deafening.

'Got to go, Nana. See you on Monday.'

'Hang in there, pumpkin. Whatever it is, we'll handle it together.'

When Emily sat up, her appetite had returned and she demolished the whole sandwich before remembering that the bacon had been meant for Lotta.

🐾

The chicken was cold in Emily's hand as she crept out into the courtyard late that night. She'd had to make herself stay awake – by pinching herself and making up scary stories about ghosts in the walls – until Dad went up to bed. He had taken forever to put his light out. It was nearly midnight, and the moon gave the snow a bluish look.

She had her panda blanket wrapped around her shoulders, and in her pocket was an alarm clock.

'Lotta?' The door creaked open and a thin beam of light from Emily's torch picked out the familiar shape of the lynx pressed against the wall. Only this time, she didn't bother to stand up. She gave a half-hearted hiss and stayed hunched where she was.

A sick feeling swam over Emily. Was Lotta ill? She hadn't had much to eat today, and it did smell really bad in the outhouse.

Emily opened the packet of chicken and tipped it on to the ground. Lotta didn't move, so Emily nudged it closer with her toe.

'Come on,' she whispered. 'You need to eat.' She pulled out a bottle of water from her pocket and poured it into the empty ice cream tub. 'Maybe you need a drink?'

Lotta didn't respond.

Emily leaned against the wall and let herself slide slowly down until she was sitting. Wrapping herself in the panda blanket, she settled into the comfiest position she could find on the cold concrete floor. 'Maybe you're scared of the dark? Don't worry, Lotta. I'll stay with you tonight.'

She set the alarm clock to go off at half past four in the morning – so she could make sure she was back in bed well before Dad woke up – and switched off the torch in case it was scaring Lotta. She tried to relax and not think about the spiders scuttling about in corners.

'*I'm not scared of the silly old dark,*' she crooned, half to Lotta and half to herself.

'*I'm safe and it can't hurt me.*

One small light will scare it away…'

She delved into her other pocket and found Josie's star.

'*And bring Nana Godwin to me,*' she breathed.

Emily let her head fall back against the wall. Her feet were cold already, and she'd only been out here a few minutes. Pulling them in under the panda blanket, she huddled into a tight ball and tried to go to sleep. But all she could think about were her feet. Her whole mind was focused on her toes, which were not freezing exactly, but definitely not warm. She tried wiggling them, and she imagined warm blood pumping from her heart all the way down her legs into her toes. She pictured them as fat grapes hanging on a tree in hot sunshine.

None of it worked.

Then, through her huffing and puffing and sighing, she heard … something. A small sound. A scuffle, a shuffle, a soft padding movement. She held her breath, her frozen feet forgotten in an instant.

A warm heaviness pressed against her side, pulled away again and then settled at her feet, beside the ticking clock.

'Lotta?' she whispered.

There was a tiny growl and then nothing more than the rasp of breathing in the dark.

A glow spread through Emily's body that had nothing to do with the temperature in the outhouse. 'I'm here, Lotta,' she murmured. 'You don't need to be afraid.'

And for the first time all week, she realised, as she drifted off into a doze, neither did she.

16

When the alarm clock blasted off, two things happened. One, Emily jumped and cracked her head against the wall. Two, the weight at her feet vanished, cold flooding back into the space Lotta had left behind.

Usually, once Emily was awake, she was wide awake. But this time her whole body wanted to pull her back down into sleep. Too stiff to bother moving anything; too drowsy to think about sitting up. She was vaguely aware of her pulse swooshing in her ears. So slow tonight, slower than the click of the tock … the clock of the tick… Her brain wouldn't form any proper thoughts.

Sleep. Go back to sleep.

No. Something was nudging her, pressing against her side. Whiskers against her face.

She had to wake up. But it was cold, so very cold…

Must sleep.

'Ow!' A sharp nip on her ear brought her back. And another. 'Ow! Stop it!'

Emily forced herself to roll over and grope for her torch, but she couldn't find it. It must have rolled away. It was so dark that she couldn't see her hand in front of her face. The glow of the star wasn't much use for actually seeing anything. It just made her fingers look green and pale, like alien fingers.

Another nip, on her hand this time. The panda blanket had slipped from her shoulders and the cold was seeping through her down jacket.

Got to move. Got to get out of here. Warm.

Emily fumbled her way to the door. She inched her hand upwards until she found the latch, lifted and pushed. Nothing happened. She pushed again, but it wouldn't budge. It felt like there was a heavy weight on the other side, blocking it.

A violent shiver took hold of Emily and shook her body. Her teeth began to chatter. She couldn't stop them, no matter how hard she tried. She sat in front of the door, her limbs heavy and numb, her head bowed.

Nip. Nip. It was like being stabbed by invisible needles in the dark. 'Leave me, Lotta. Let me sleep.' *Nip.*

Can't stay here. Someone will find us in the

morning. Find Lotta. The thought rose to the surface of her mind like bubbles pushing against an iced-over pond.

Got to get the door open. Push, Em, push.

She let her full body weight fall against the door and pressed the flat of her hands against it, feeling the strain in her shoulders. The door budged a little bit. Emily was shivering so hard she could hardly control her movements.

Push again.

She pushed and Lotta nipped at her, and each time the door gave a little bit, and then a little more, until there was a gap wide enough for Emily to get her hand through. Her knee knocked against the torch, rolling around on the floor, and she managed to get hold of it. Her fingers were so cold they wouldn't work properly, but at last she managed to flick it on.

Snow. The doorway was blocked with snow, as high as her knees would be if she had the energy to stand up.

Dig. Got to dig.

She drove her fingers into the snow over and over. The pink fleecy gloves that Nana Godwin had given her last Christmas were worse than useless, soaked within seconds. Her fingers ached and burned with the cold. Again and again, she drove her hand into the snow, scooping it away and reaching round the back of the door to clear a bit of a space.

The door moved, just enough to let her slip through, if she could only stand up. At the last moment, she remembered the star. She must take it with her, just in case … just in case…

She couldn't remember why. All she knew was that the star was important.

Lotta pressed against her, trying to ease herself through the gap.

'No, no. You've got to stay here,' said Emily, though she couldn't remember why that was either, or why the two of them were out here in the first place. She got to her hands and knees and crawled through the space, making herself as thin as possible, and shutting the door with her foot the moment she was free.

Outside, she rolled over on to her back and lay in the snow, arms and legs spread out like an angel. Fat, feathery flakes poured out of the sky. She had never seen so much snow. It was like someone up there was shaking out a feather duvet over her. Perhaps it was Mum; was she up there, looking down at her baby and trying to cover her, to keep her warm? Because it *was* surprisingly warm now. She had even stopped shivering and there was no more pain from her fingers. She couldn't feel them at all.

Everything was okay now. Lotta was safe in the outhouse. Emily was warm out here. She would just have a little sleep and then think about going indoors.

Her eyes closed and she drifted away.

🐾

Someone was crying again. Jagged, gulping sobs. But it sounded closer this time, not behind the wall. Emily's eyes flickered open. There was white above her, and a cold, wintry light in the room. She flexed her fingers. Where was she?

'Emily?' Josie's voice, filled with concern. But Emily didn't feel like talking, so she closed her eyes again. She wanted that feeling back – that Christmassy, snow-angel feeling – but it had all gone, like warm water down a plughole, leaving her cold and exposed in an empty bath.

The crying stopped abruptly. 'She's awake?' Warm skin against her forehead, a rough hand. 'Emily? It's Dad here.' This time she opened her eyes properly, and there he was, attempting to smile but only managing a horrid grimace. 'How are you doing?' He took her hand and chafed her fingers. 'Can you feel this?' He pressed each of her fingernails and Emily knew he was checking to see how quickly the blood flowed back underneath them; he had showed her how to do it once when she had a chest infection.

She pulled her hand away. How could she begin to explain how she had felt out in the snow, how she felt now? She turned over, face to the wall.

'Maybe take her temperature again?' Josie suggested. 'If it's still on the low side, we really should take her to hospital and get her checked over.'

Emily felt her arm being lifted and the chill of a thermometer as Dad popped it under her arm. She hoped it wasn't the same one he put up dogs' bottoms.

'Thirty-six-point-five,' said Dad. 'It's almost normal. But can you go and find another blanket, just to be on the safe side? I think there's one on a shelf in the top of my wardrobe.'

Josie padded across the corridor and into Dad's bedroom. 'Can't find one,' she called. 'Tell you what, I'll nip over to my studio and get a couple of hot-water bottles. It gets really cold in there sometimes and I use them to warm my hands up when I'm painting.' She went downstairs and Emily heard the back door opening and closing.

Dad leaned over and rested his cheek on Emily's shoulder.

'I was so worried about you,' he said. 'You could have died.'

She didn't respond.

'Em? Speak to me. Tell me how you're feeling. Let me help.'

'I don't think you can.' Her voice came out in a fragile miaow, like Alexander's, and she had to wipe away a tear. 'I just want Mum back.'

'Oh darling, so do I.'

Perhaps it was the *darling* or simply the need for a warm pair of arms, but Emily turned all of a sudden and buried her face in Dad's neck.

'It's all right,' he said. 'We don't have to do this, you know.'

Emily stiffened. What did he mean?

'Maybe I should never have brought you here,' he went on. 'We can go home if you like, or we can both live with Grandma Underwood. I can see it's too much for you and I'm beginning to think it's too much for me, too.'

Emily rolled away from him and lay on her back, letting the white painted ceiling of her little bedroom swim into focus. So much depended on what she said now.

'I want to stay here.'

'Are you just saying that? Because I know it must

have been hard leaving your home, your friends, just because I couldn't cope with it all – couldn't face Christmas on our own. We can pack up today and leave. Rufus will understand. He can find someone else to take his daughter's place.'

'But Nana Godwin is coming for Christmas.'

Dad took hold of Emily's hand again and squeezed it tight.

'No, Emily. She's not.'

'What do you mean?' A fresh sob rose in Emily's throat, blocking it so that she couldn't breathe. She sat up, her head swimming. 'Of course she's coming. She promised.'

Nana Godwin *had* to come. Who else would tell Emily what to do? She reached for her panda blanket, but it wasn't there.

'The trains are cancelled because of the snow. She can't come.'

17

More snow fell, but Emily barely noticed. The Christmas tree stood, bare and forlorn, in a corner of the living room, dropping needles already. Grandma Underwood would definitely not approve. She only allowed fake trees in her house, and they didn't smell the same. Someone should water it.

Emily lay on the saggy sofa, burrowed under a duvet, staring at the ceiling, and Dad slouched on the armchair, doing the same thing. Neither of them spoke. Occasionally, Dad sighed, but he never moved.

'I could have lost you too,' he said at last. All the anger was gone, leaving his voice thin and faint, like the wind whistling through the broken windows of an empty house.

'Who found me?'

'Josie. Don't ask me why she was out and about at

that time of the morning – said she couldn't sleep, so she came down to the studio to do some painting. And there you were, unconscious in the snow. You must have been sleepwalking; it's quite common when kids are stressed. Lots of little cuts and scratches on you, and you had this in your hand.' He held up the star, not glowing now, just a bundle of twigs tied together. 'Shall I put it on the tree?' He made no move to get up, just stared at it blankly.

'No. I want it.' Emily wriggled her arms out from beneath the duvet and held out her hands. Dad threw the star and she caught it.

Another silence fell. Outside the window, the flakes continued to fall. Perhaps they would just keep falling and falling, and this little cottage would be completely buried. They could hide away here, just her and Dad, and nobody would ever find them again.

A loud knock at the front door made them jump. It opened and Rufus Hardacre stood on the doorstep, shedding snow on to the floor. Jacky nipped in behind him and snuffled around the living room, his nose to the carpet.

'Just here to inform you,' said Rufus, 'that you may expect a visit from the police later on.'

'The police?' Emily sat up, the duvet slipping on to the floor.

Rufus swivelled his eyes towards her, though he kept his body stiffly to attention. 'Looking for that stolen lynx kitten. They're checking sheds, garages, outhouses and suchlike. They want to talk to you, Underwood, since you saw the carcass of the mother.'

Carcass. What a horrible word. It made her sound like a slab of meat in the butcher's shop.

The thought of meat reminded Emily that she not only needed to feed Lotta, but to replace the chicken she'd taken from the fridge last night. There had been no chance to do it all day. Dad had called the doctor out in the end, and he had ordered her to have a quiet day and stay warm. But after a whole morning and half the afternoon huddled on the sofa, she was desperate to see Lotta somehow and get her panda blanket back. And it would be dark soon; most of the day had already gone.

A hot flush swept over her. She'd been counting on Nana Godwin to help her carry this heavy secret, and to help her figure out what on earth to do. Now there was nobody.

She stood up and heaved herself on to the staircase so she could get upstairs without having to pass anywhere near Rufus. She crawled up on all fours and stayed on her hands and knees when she reached the landing, just because it seemed easier and somehow safer to stay close to the ground. When she reached her bedroom, she scrambled up on to the bed with all the energy of a weary sloth and slumped there, her legs too heavy to lift. She held the star at arm's length, against the backdrop of the snow-filled sky, framed by the window.

It had brought help last night, hadn't it? Not the help she wanted – *Josie*, of all people – but help, at least. Slowly, she got on to her knees and reached up to the curtain rail above the window. She looped the star over the rail by its golden thread, so it hung there, twirling and twisting in the breeze that somehow managed to get through the closed window.

Downstairs, the front door slammed. She saw Rufus come out and stamp down the lane to his own gate next door. He wanted them to leave. Dad wanted to leave. Nana Godwin wasn't coming, so what was there to stay for?

She thought of the warm weight of Lotta leaning against her last night, and the nipping teeth that had helped her to stay awake and get out of the outhouse. She couldn't leave now. She had to protect Lotta, no matter what happened. And first of all, that meant feeding her.

She felt slow, warm energy creep back into her body and she half climbed, half jumped off the bed, landing with a thud on the floor. Keeping her pyjamas on, she piled more clothes on top.

'Dad? Can I go outside for a while? I've got loads of layers on, and I'm really warm.'

'No.' Dad was back in the armchair, staring at the ceiling, his hands laced behind his head.

'But I think I must have taken my panda blanket with me when I went … um … sleepwalking.'

'Just leave it, Em. Doctor's orders.'

'But Dad, it's my *panda blanket*.'

When she was younger, she had left it at the playground in the local park, and they hadn't realised until bedtime. Dad had gone out in the dark, into the park that was spooky at night and had all kinds of people hanging around it, like teenagers and bogeymen, and he had rescued the panda blanket. Surely he must understand? If not, she'd have to lay it on thick.

'I can't sleep without it, and especially today I really, really need it because Nana Godwin isn't coming and…' She was making herself properly upset and she wasn't having to pretend. She definitely did need it.

Dad heaved a sigh. 'All right. Five minutes. In the courtyard only. Then you come straight back in again.'

Emily dashed for the kitchen door.

'Em?'

'Yes?'

'Put a hat on.'

She grabbed her red bobble hat from the kitchen bench and went to the coat hooks behind the door. 'My coat's wet.'

'Put mine on.'

Emily pulled Dad's coat down by yanking it until it slid off its hook. She slid herself into it and disappeared into a delicious hiding place that smelled of him. She turned up the collar so that it covered her ears, and pulled the sleeves back so she could get hold of the door handle.

'I'll shut this door to keep the heat in,' she announced. Just what Mum had always said.

Dad grunted, and Emily shut him in the living room with his thoughts so she could scurry to the fridge and grab a packet of ham. She would make sure to ask for cheese next time they had sandwiches, and hope that Dad would have the same.

Outside, the snow had stopped falling and a weak wash of late afternoon sunlight lit everything. The welcome owl wore a huge hat of snow. There was no sign of what had happened last night. It was a clean page, ready to be started again.

Glancing round to make sure that nobody was watching, Emily dug away some of the snow against the outhouse door and opened it. The reek of the air inside hit her in the face, but she didn't dare to open the door fully. Instead, she reached in and felt for the edge of the panda blanket, which was damp and stiff with cold. She eased it out through the gap. She peeled open the packet of ham and threw in all six slices.

'Back later, Lotta,' she whispered, pressing her eye to the crack in the door.

But Lotta didn't respond. Not a growl, not a hiss. She was lying at the back of the outhouse and didn't even lift her head when Emily spoke. Her ribcage rose and fell quickly, as though she had just finished chasing a deer.

'Lotta?' Was she just asleep, or was she getting sick?

'What are you up to, hmm?'

Emily jumped, and pushed the door to. It wouldn't quite shut properly. She managed to close it enough to secure it with the hook, but the hook seemed loose, as though it was coming out of the wall. Rufus must have come into the courtyard through the gate in his backyard when she wasn't looking. How much had he seen? How much had he heard?

'What are you hiding in there, girl?' He took a step

towards her, the snow over the top of his lace-up boots.

She stood with her back to the outhouse door, praying that Lotta would stay quiet.

'Just … um … checking the outhouse. You know, like you said. To save the police doing it.'

As she spoke, Jacky came racing out to join them, the white bits of his fur looking dirty yellow against the fresh snow. He yipped and yelped, bounding about with excitement until he almost disappeared into a snowdrift. He wriggled out, shook himself off and began sniffing around the door of the outhouse.

'What is it, Jacky? What's in there, hmm?' Rufus took another step closer.

'It's nothing,' said Emily, desperately. 'He's just sniffing my blanket. I … it needs a wash.' She shoved the panda blanket in Jacky's face and he went half-crazy at the scent of Lotta's wee. 'See? That's all it is. There's nothing in the outhouse. I've checked.'

Jacky left the blanket alone and went back to sniffing round the outhouse, growling as he went.

'Hmmm. Perhaps I should see for myself.' Rufus's hand went to the hook on the door.

'No!' gasped Emily.

'Move aside, girl. I want to see what's in there that's making Jacky so excited.'

'Hey, Soup.' It was Dibs, standing at the gate. 'Wotcha doing? Want to come and see Alexander?'

Emily clenched her fists as though she could keep all the complications hidden inside them. She wanted more than anything to go and sit in the farmhouse kitchen again and tickle Alexander's cute white tummy. But Dibs would want to know what she wanted to talk to him about, and she couldn't tell him about Lotta, knowing how he felt about the lynx. Plus, if she went to the farm, what would stop Rufus poking about in the outhouse while she was gone?

'Emily?' The back door opened and Dad came out. 'You've had your five minutes and I see you've found your blanket. Time to come in now.'

'But...'

'No buts. I'm not taking any risks with your health, not after last night. You're staying in the warm and no arguments.'

Rufus took his hand off the hook. 'Last night? What happened last night?'

'Nothing that concerns you,' said Dad with an icy politeness.

'I'll be the judge of what concerns me,' snapped Rufus. 'Now, I have an appointment to keep.' He whistled to Jacky and set off, striding over the snow.

Emily let out a long, slow breath. Dibs was still hovering at the gate.

'I'm not allowed today,' she said, feeling a rush of something like gratitude towards Dad for making the decision for her.

Dibs looked disappointed. 'Maybe tomorrow?'

Emily hesitated. If she stayed in the farmhouse kitchen with everyone else around, then Dibs wouldn't be able to ask any private questions, would he? She could have some hot chocolate and cake, play with Alexander and then come home again.

'Yeah, all right. Tomorrow.'

Dibs gave her a thumbs up and a big grin, then trotted away, his boots scrunching in the snow.

'You found your panda blanket, then?' said Dad. She'd forgotten she was holding it until now. 'Where was it?'

'Just ... lying about. I must have brought it out here from my bed. I'll just put it ... um...' Where should she put it? Not back on the bed, that was for sure, not smelling the way it did. 'In the wash.'

She ducked her head, but she had to pass right by Dad to get into the kitchen, and he wrinkled his nose as she passed. He caught her by the shoulders.

'Emily, look at me. It's nothing to be ashamed of,

you know. It's quite normal, in the circumstances, but it is a bit of an alarm bell for me.'

'What?' She hadn't the faintest clue what he was talking about.

'Wetting the bed.' He bent so that his forehead was resting against hers, allowing him to speak in a low, confiding voice. 'I thought you were doing okay with it all – better than me, at any rate – but I see now that you're not. Wetting the bed, sleepwalking, wandering off. It's all a cry for help, isn't it?'

He thought that *she* had wet the panda blanket. At her age! And now she would have to pretend that she had, because she couldn't give him the real explanation, could she?

'I'll talk to someone. Get you some more counselling.'

What was the point? She could go to a hundred of those sessions, sitting in that cramped room with the kind lady and her massive, magnified eyes, but it wouldn't bring Mum back. She wanted to give the right answers to all the questions. And she desperately wanted someone to tell her how to get rid of the cold feeling she got when the faceless monster began to creep up on her again. But she had far more important things to worry about. Like getting Lotta's outhouse cleaned up properly and making sure that

135

Rufus didn't find out there was a lynx hiding on his property.

And finding out who had shot Lotta's mother. Was it Granger, or was it Rufus? There must be some way of finding out whether Rufus used the red gun cartridges as well. An idea began to form in her mind, though she didn't know if she was brave enough to carry it through.

'I'm fine,' she said, even though that wasn't strictly true. She wriggled out of Dad's grip and went over to the washing machine. She shoved the panda blanket in, poured in some washing powder and turned the dial to 'on'. That was yet another thing she'd had to learn in the last six months. Before, Mum had always done the washing and it came out soft and fluffy and sweet-smelling. Now it always ended up quite stiff and hard, and it never smelled the same.

She twiddled with the dial a bit more. Nothing happened. 'I think it's broken.'

Dad swore. 'Great. That's all I need.' He messed about with the controls, gave it a kick and fiddled about a bit more. Nothing. 'Hang on a minute.' He flicked the light switch on and off, but nothing happened. 'The clock on the microwave's out, too. We've got a power cut.'

He was right. None of the lights would come on, nor the television.

'We'll have to sort it out later,' he said.

'But I need to wash it now, or it won't dry in time for bed.' The thought was unbearable.

'There isn't time. Look, don't get upset about it. Don't ... don't cry, Em. We can wash it by hand in the sink. Then I'll make a roaring fire and we'll hang it up to dry.'

She hadn't meant the tears to leak out, she really hadn't. It had just been a long and exhausting night, on top of a long and exhausting week, on top of a long and exhausting six months. The crumpled panda blanket squashed into a washing machine that wouldn't even work just seemed to top it all off. No matter how she tried, the tears wouldn't stop coming.

It wasn't the kind of deep, jerky sobbing that she knew so well, nor the throat-filling, nose-swelling, headache-making kind of crying where she wanted to let it all out but it just got stuck inside her face. This time, she just went quietly about her business while the tears got on with pouring.

And she let them. What was the point of doing anything else? It was all hopeless – Mum, Nana Godwin, Dibs, Lotta – everything was just too wrong to fix.

Around lunchtime the next day, Dad's phone rang. Emily had spent another morning confined to the cottage and she was desperate to go out.

'I need to go to the farm,' said Dad. 'Problem with one of the sheep, and the other vet is stuck in snow, so I need to go. It's not something I want you to see, so I'll give Josie a call and see if she's around to keep an eye on you.'

'I can stay here by myself,' protested Emily. 'Josie's got work to do. She must be sick of having to look after me, especially when I *don't* need it. I'm not a baby.'

'Maybe not, but you're still my daughter. You had a nasty experience yesterday, Em. You could have died.' That was the second time he'd said that.

'But I'm fine now. Look.' She got up and did five star jumps in the middle of the living room.

'Even so.' Dad called Josie's number and Emily heard the click and Josie's voice at the other end. They had a quick conversation and then Dad hung up. 'She's in the village, picking up some supplies.'

'You can leave me,' Emily insisted.

'Normally, I would,' said Dad. 'But after yesterday

... let's just say I feel better knowing that someone – an adult – is with you. Come on.'

Emily knew when his mind was made up.

'What's wrong at the farm?' she asked, putting on her jacket, which had been hanging on the wooden airer in front of the fire. It was like putting on a warm cloud.

'One of the sheep has been savaged.'

'Savaged?'

'Something has chased it and attacked it. It's not going to be pleasant, so you can stay out of the way.'

Dad picked up the battered leather bag that had all his vet stuff in it: medicines, prescription pads, a stethoscope and all kinds of other interesting stuff. Emily had got into trouble plenty of times for taking things out of it to make her toy animals better.

'Right,' he said grimly. 'Let's see what's what.'

Footprints criss-crossed the farmyard. Heaps of manure yellowed the snow and wisps of straw blew about in the rising wind.

'Hello?' called Dad. 'Anybody home?'

He went to the door of the farmhouse and knocked. There was no answer.

'Nobody knocks here, remember?' said Emily, pushing past him.

She went straight into the kitchen, which was deliciously warm and smelled of baking bread. She went to the lower oven of the Aga and opened it. There was Alexander, fast asleep. He opened his eyes and gave a miaow, showing the pink of his tongue.

'I'll stay here,' said Emily, scooping him out. He had grown some more and filled both her cupped hands.

'Not on your own, you won't.' Dad, who had followed her in, took the kitten and put him back in the oven. 'Sorry, little chap.'

'I'm not a chap,' protested Emily.

'I wasn't talking to you.' Dad was already halfway out of the door. Emily saw that more snow was falling outside. It reminded her all over again that Nana Godwin wasn't coming, and a rock settled in her stomach.

The two of them crossed the yard, hoods pulled up against the snowflakes that whirled about in the wind. Streak exploded from the tractor shed, barking like mad.

'Streak, it's just me,' said Emily, holding out her hand. Streak stood her ground, tail pressed hard between her back legs, lips pulled back.

'Watch it, or she might nip you. She makes a good guard dog.' Dad pushed Emily behind him so that he was between her and Streak. 'But you have to let them know who's boss. Don't show any fear.'

He kept talking in a low murmur as he and Emily inched past Streak towards the field gate.

'Dibs says she used to be such a friendly thing,' Emily said. 'Something must have hurt her very badly to behave like that. But she's absolutely brilliant with the sheep.'

At last Streak seemed to be satisfied that they weren't a threat, and slunk back to the tractor shed. She vanished into the dark hole beneath the tractor and Emily imagined her there, flakes of red paint falling on her face like bloody snow.

In the field, Dibs and Sal crouched in a huddle in the corner where two hedges met. The hedges were twisted and bent, leaning as though the wind had blown them out of shape. They reminded Emily of witches, all bony and twiggy.

Nessie and Bean were amusing Flump at the other end of the field, rolling an enormous ball of snow to make a snowman.

'Go and join them.' Dad nudged her.

'But I want to see.' Emily was too anxious to play, plus she wanted to see what was going on.

'It's not suitable.' Dad was opening his bag as he walked, pulling out his stethoscope.

'Dibs is here, and he's the same age as me.' She knew that wasn't true, but it sounded convincing.

'No, I'm not,' growled Dibs, his face creased with worry. 'I'm way older than you, Soup. I'm nearly thirteen.'

'Em, I'm not going to argue with you,' said Dad, even though he was already arguing with her.

It didn't matter anyway. Dibs and Sal straightened up and stepped to one side, and Emily saw what lay between them. A sheep staring at the wintry sky without seeing anything, its throat ripped. It was still panting and twitching, its legs jerking. But as Dad crouched to examine it, the jerking stopped and the panting got slower and slower.

'I'm sorry,' said Dad. 'There's nothing I can do here.'

'Now you know why I hate those lynx,' stormed Dibs. 'Look what they've done!'

'Steady on.' Dad snapped on a pair of surgical gloves and took a close look at the sheep, which lay still, staring glassy-eyed at the sky. 'You don't know that. It could have been something else.'

'A fox?' said Emily, taking the opportunity to creep closer.

'A fox wouldn't be able to take down a fully-grown ewe,' said Dad. 'Not big enough, especially at this time of year when food is scarce.'

'But if it was hungry enough…?'

'More likely a dog.' Dad peered at the snow around the sheep, dusting it with his fingers. His hood had fallen away and there were big flakes in his hair. 'Seen any strange dogs running around out here?'

'No,' said Dibs. 'Streak would let us know if there was another dog around.'

'Don't go trying to blame this on a dog.' Sal threw out her arms, her face twisted with fury. 'We know what's done this and I'm sick of it all. Sick of worrying and sick of watching and…'

There was a bump and a wail from the children, and she was instantly alert. Nessie and Bean were stuffing snow into Flump's hood and then pulling it up so it went all over his head. 'Those kids'll be the death of me, I swear.' She stomped over to sort them out, leaving Dibs to face Dad and Emily.

'That's it,' he said, his face as surly as the first day Emily had spotted him. No trace of a smile now. 'I'm getting Dad's shotgun out and if I see one of those lynx, I'm going to shoot it.'

Emily's stomach did a somersault. Surely he didn't mean it? This was *Dibs*, her friend. But how could she

143

be friends with someone who would say such a horrible thing?

'You can't!' she said. 'They're just innocent animals.'

'Innocent animals? I don't think an innocent animal did that.' He pointed at the sheep's bloody throat. 'You don't know what you're talking about, so why don't you just butt out?'

'She's right,' said Dad. 'You can't shoot the lynx. For one, it's against the law, and for two, you're just a kid and you don't have a licence to handle a firearm.'

'Just a kid, am I?' Dibs spat into the snow. 'I've been shooting rabbits since I was this high.' He held his hand out level with his knee.

'What, since you were born?' spluttered Emily.

Dibs came over, lifting his boots high to get through the snow, and pushed his face right up against hers. 'Better watch out, *Emily*,' he hissed so that Dad, crouching by the sheep, couldn't hear, 'or I might just mistake you for a lynx and shoot you as well.'

Emily knew he was just upset. That people said stupid things when they were hurting. But he was supposed to be her friend, wasn't he? She wanted to flinch away from him, from the harshness in his eyes, but she stood her ground, hugging to her the secret knowledge that Lotta, at least, was safe in the outhouse.

For now. She might not be safe for much longer unless Emily found some help. Her gaze drifted towards Dad's bag, where he'd left it open on the ground. He kept some medicines in there. Perhaps she could just…

Dad closed the bag with a snap.

Suddenly, she needed to see Lotta. To check that she was okay, that nobody – Rufus or the police or anyone else – was sniffing around the outhouse.

'Dad, can I go home now?'

'In a minute. There's not much I can do here. You can sort out what needs doing?' he said to Dibs.

Dibs gave Emily one last glare before stepping away. 'Course I will. I know what I have to do.'

'I need to go *now*,' said Emily.

'I said, in a minute!'

Emily folded her arms and pouted. 'But I'm so *cold*,' she said, even though she was pretty toasty inside her coat. 'I don't feel very well.' She tried to make her teeth chatter but they wouldn't.

Dad snatched up his bag and peeled off his gloves. 'Why didn't you say so? Come on, let's get you into the warm.'

Emily followed the hedge back to the gate, but it

was slow going because snow had begun to drift and it was over the top of her wellies. Once in the farmyard, she raced ahead of Dad down the lane and back to the cottage. Straight through the gate at the back, into the courtyard.

There was no sign of Rufus or the police, thank goodness.

But the hook from the outhouse door lay in the snow.

And the door was open.

18

The rock in Emily's stomach dropped right down into her boots, weighing down her feet so that she couldn't move.

If the door was open, then Lotta must be out. If Lotta was out, she couldn't be far away because she had definitely been in there half an hour ago when they had left for the farm. She would be easy to spot in broad daylight, and if Dibs kept his word and got a shotgun out, she would be an easy target.

But what if Rufus had found her? What would he have done with her?

Think, she told herself. *Look at the evidence.* Had Lotta escaped, or had someone let her out? There were dints in the snow all over the courtyard. Small paw marks and large, human ones. Fresh snow had fallen on them all, smoothing the edges, hiding the shapes. She and Dad, Rufus and Jacky had all walked here earlier. But what about Lotta?

At the outhouse door, there was a scraped area in the snow, where the door had been pushed open, just wide enough for a lynx kitten to escape. And there were more paw prints, clear and fresh, coming out into the snow. They must have been made very recently because the snow hadn't covered them yet. There were no fresh human prints, which meant that Lotta must have escaped on her own.

Emily let out a breath, feeling as limp as a burst balloon. Nobody had let Lotta out. But, she realised with a fresh burst of panic, if Lotta had only just escaped, she must be nearby and Dad was only...

'Em?'

Dad was back. And he wasn't alone. Granger, of all people, stood behind him, squinting around in his usual sullen way. Quickly, she scuffed snow over the paw prints, trying to hide them. Hopefully Dad would just think they were Jacky's prints from earlier.

'Look who I found hanging about,' said Dad, nodding at Granger. 'He wants to know about the lynx, whether the police have any leads.'

'The missing one?' squeaked Emily.

'The shot one,' growled Granger, glaring at her.

'And have they?'

148

Dad shook his head. 'Nothing yet. But someone must know something about one or the other. All it takes is one person with some information, some evidence, and we'll get to the bottom of this, you'll see.'

Information. Evidence. Like blankets, ice cream tubs and alarm clocks? All the things that were in the outhouse just metres from where they stood.

'In you come then,' said Dad. 'Let's get you warmed up.'

Her eyes flickered towards Granger, who was peering at the snow and frowning. He took a step closer to the outhouse and seemed to be looking at the ground.

'I want to stay outside.' She had to get Granger away from the outhouse and clear her stuff away before anyone got a chance to look inside.

She needed to find out where Lotta had gone, to try and follow her paw prints before the snow covered them completely.

'No. Absolutely not. You said you were cold, so you're coming indoors and you're staying there for the rest of the day.'

She needed an excuse not to go in yet. 'Can't I just go and see if Josie's in? I need to … um … say thank you. For finding me last night.'

Dad looked doubtful. 'Okay, then. But I'm coming with you.'

She had no choice but to walk over to the studio, Dad shadowing her every step. The welcome owl looked unusually smug today, almost hidden in a hooded cloak of thick snow. She swiped it off as she passed. Let it feel the chill like everyone else.

Inside, the light was greenish, filtered through a row of old glass bottles in a high-up window. Emily decided that she preferred the white light outside. Everything in here looked seasick, with dark shadows in the corners. And it was cold enough to grow icicles on your nose. Clearly there was no electricity here, either.

'Josie?' called Dad.

A commotion started in the back room: the sound of a stool crashing to the ground.

'Josie? Are you all right?'

The sliding door made a grinding noise as it opened, and Josie appeared. Today she was wearing an oversized grey fleece hoodie. She looked like a squirrel. Her hair was all over the place and she was panting, as though she'd been running. There was a streak of blood along her forearm where her sleeve was rolled up.

Emily's eyes widened. Josie's met hers and signalled urgently, *Say nothing.*

'What's going on back there?' Dad stepped forward. 'Have you got a problem?'

'No, no, it's fine.' Josie pressed her hand against his chest to stop him. 'I was just … moving some furniture around.' There was another crash. 'Oh, that's just … silly me, I shouldn't have stacked things so high.'

'Come on, Em,' said Dad. 'Say thank you and then we'll get out of here.'

'Actually, perhaps she could stay and … well, *help* me?' Josie gave Emily a meaningful look.

Emily nodded vigorously. 'Yes, I could, couldn't I, Dad? You know, as a way of saying thank you. To Josie.'

There was a thud and the sound of something scrabbling.

Josie gave an unconvincing laugh. 'Ha-ha. My … er … my sister's dog. I'm looking after it for a few days. It's a bit bonkers.' She tittered and twirled a forefinger in the air beside her head.

'Not the only one,' Dad muttered to himself as he headed for the door. Then he stopped and turned round. 'Wait a minute. A dog, you say? Has it been out of your sight today?'

'No.'

'It couldn't have been to the farm? Can I see it?'

151

Emily felt panic rising. 'I think Josie would know if her dog had escaped, Dad.'

He rolled his shoulders as though they felt tight. 'You're right. I'm sorry. Just makes me so mad when people don't control their animals properly.' He shot an embarrassed look at Josie. 'I don't mean you, of course. I mean… Never mind. Just send my daughter back to me when you're done.' He ducked towards the door again. 'If you're sure you feel okay, Em, I think I might go and boil up some water on the gas cooker and have a shave.' He rubbed his bristles. 'Try and make myself human again.'

'Of course.' Emily stood beside Josie with a grin fixed to her face. 'Bye, Dad,' she said. 'We'll be fine.'

The door closed. Both of them scrambled for the back room.

'Have you got her?' gasped Emily.

Josie put her hand on the door. 'Stand back.'

She slid open the door and there, crouching in a pile of fallen and clawed canvases, the stool lying beside her, was Lotta. Her eyes glowed amber in the snowy glare from the skylight, but her coat looked dull. Not smooth and glossy, like it had when she was free.

'Isn't she beautiful?' whispered Josie, bending forward, her hands resting on her thighs. 'I went outside for a few minutes to feed the birds and left the door open. She just walked in. Then she panicked and I managed to herd her in here.'

'She escaped from the outhouse. But she's mine. I'm taking care of her.'

'You can't take care of a wild animal without proper facilities,' murmured Josie. 'It's not fair on the animal.'

'I'm doing all right,' said Emily through gritted teeth. There was no way she was going to say thank you to Josie for anything. 'I feed her and give her water and keep her clean.'

'She doesn't look well,' said Josie. 'She needs her freedom.'

'She needs her *mother*,' insisted Emily, 'but her mother is dead. If she goes out there, she has no one to look after her. I'm putting her back in the outhouse and you can't stop me.'

'Hello, there! Anybody home, hmmm?'

They both froze.

Heavy feet clumped about in the next room, stopping every now and then as Rufus picked something up, harrumphed at it and put it back down with a slight scrape.

'I'd better go,' whispered Josie, straightening up. She wagged a finger in Emily's face. 'But this is not over. Stay here.' She went through to the studio, sliding the door shut behind her.

Emily sat down on the floor. 'It's only me, Lotta,' she said in a sing-song voice. 'You've got nothing to worry about.'

The lynx seemed to relax a little, her ears flicking back and forth as the sound of other voices drifted through the door.

'No, no...' That was Josie's voice, its higher pitch easier to hear. 'The *outhouse*? No, I don't...'

Emily stiffened and tried to listen more closely. Did that mean Rufus had looked inside the outhouse?

'...people like that Granger sniffing around the place...' Rufus rumbled on.

She shivered. If either of them had seen inside, they would know that someone had kept an animal in there. She wondered what the police did to children who were caught breaking the law. Would they send her away to prison? She hadn't meant to be bad, only to help Lotta.

'...should keep it locked...' Josie went on. 'Yes, a bolt on it...' Sounded like she was getting a tongue-lashing from old Rufus.

Emily wriggled uncomfortably on the cold concrete floor. Perhaps she *did* have something to thank Josie for, after all.

A couple of minutes later, Josie came back, her cheeks flushed pink. She was carrying a stethoscope.

'You owe me one,' she said. 'Oh, and Rufus gave me this.' She tapped the stethoscope. 'It's your dad's. He left it at the farm.'

'But how did Rufus get it?'

'That boy from the farm – what's his name? Dobs?'

'Dibs.'

'That's it. He brought it round. He was in a bit of a hurry, Rufus said. Didn't want to hang around.'

'He could have knocked at the cottage.'

Josie shrugged. 'Maybe he did, and your dad didn't hear. He said he was going to have a shave, didn't he?'

Or maybe Dibs just didn't want to see us, thought Emily sadly.

'Now,' Josie went on, putting the stethoscope down, 'this lynx kitten has to go back where it belongs.' Emily opened her mouth to protest, but Josie wouldn't listen. 'We are going to get this pussycat out of here and back into the forest. And if you won't help me, then I'll go and get your dad, who will.'

Emily closed her mouth again. Part of her ached with misery at the thought of sending Lotta back out into the big wide world on her own. But further in and deeper down, in the place where she kept her most secret feelings, she was glad. Glad that someone else was taking charge, was making the decisions.

She nodded meekly. 'But how will we get her out of here without anyone seeing? Plus...' she sat bolt upright, '...if we just let her out and Dibs sees her, he'll shoot her. Or Rufus will.'

Or Granger. If she could only find out for sure which of them had killed Lotta's mother. Whoever had done it, it was much more wrong than helping a kitten with nobody to protect it. And they couldn't tell on her if she knew something about them.

Edging carefully past Lotta, who backed away snarling, Josie fetched something from a corner of the store room. It was a large cage.

'This is where I put little girls who don't do as they're told,' she said, solemnly.

Emily blinked.

Josie flashed her a grin. 'Just kidding. Believe it or not, my sister really *does* have a dog, and I sometimes look after it here. This is its travelling cage, for the boot of the car.'

The tension in Emily's body began to slip away, as though she had taken off a heavy suit of armour. 'How are we going to get her in there? She won't just walk in.'

'How did you get her here in the first place?'

'Meat. But there's none left in the cottage, and I have to replace it all before Dad finds out, otherwise...'

'Okay, okay. Hold your horses. We can sort that out afterwards. But I'm vegetarian, so I don't have anything meaty round here.'

'Wait. I know where there might be some. Give me two minutes.'

Emily hurried outside and looked around quickly. No one in sight. The outhouse door was closed again, but the hook was gone. Without it, the door was awkward to open. With some difficulty, she wedged the tips of her fingers into the gap between the door and the frame, and pulled. A splinter of wood drove under her fingernail and she yelped. Sucking it, she peered round the door. She had hoped there might a bit of meat left in there, but there was nothing edible.

On the floor were some pieces of compacted snow in the shapes of crosses and lines. They must have been knocked out of the tread of a pair of boots – Dad had some with that distinctive pattern on the soles, but so did lots of people.

Someone had been in there. Someone must have seen the overturned ice cream tub with water in it and the soiled blanket crumpled in the corner; someone must have smelled the reek of cat wee.

Someone knew that an animal had been there, and it hadn't been trapped there by accident. Someone must know that Lotta had been kept there on purpose.

And that someone had taken Emily's alarm clock.

19

'Did you find some?' asked Josie when Emily returned to the studio.

'Find some what?' Emily had clean forgotten what she was supposed to be looking for. All she could think about was that someone had her clock. It had to be Granger – Rufus would certainly have told Josie if he'd found it. All he had to do was hand it to the police as evidence, and Emily was done for.

'Meat. For your lynx. Are you all right?'

Emily nodded, even though she was far from all right. First things first. They had to get Lotta safely back to the forest without anyone seeing her.

'Could we get some from the farm, maybe?' asked Josie, but Emily didn't really want to go back there. She didn't feel welcome any more. A little pang of self-pity hollowed out a hole beneath her heart. It had felt so comforting sitting in that warm kitchen with the family – almost as though she was part of it. But who was she kidding? She was just a stranger and they were only being kind because she'd saved Flump. That was long forgotten now, it seemed. People round here had very short memories.

'What about Rufus?' she said. 'Could you ask him?' She was far too scared to ask him herself. Besides, what if he told Dad that she'd been begging for food on his doorstep? 'Wait! Your sister's dog! Don't you have any spare tins of dog food?'

'You, my girl, are a genius.' Josie went to a low cupboard and rummaged around until she found a tin with a picture of a golden retriever on it.

She put the cage on the floor and propped open the door. She opened the tin of dog food and put some inside the cage. Lotta watched with deep suspicion, but her nostrils flared and her whiskers twitched.

'Put some close to her,' hissed Emily. 'Make a trail for her to follow.'

Josie did, and the two of them stood back against the wall. Emily crossed her fingers for good luck, and then crossed her legs for good measure.

Slowly, Lotta stood up. She kept her head down and her eyes fixed on Emily and Josie. The effort of keeping still was almost too much for Emily.

Lotta sniffed the first pile of meat. Would she eat

it? With another wary glance in Emily's direction, she licked it and then wolfed it down. The next pile was only a short distance away, and Lotta seemed to gain confidence, sitting down to savour it and licking her lips afterwards.

When she reached the cage, she sniffed it up and down, then walked right around it to sniff the back, too. Her paw snaked in through the bars, trying to get the meat inside, but she couldn't reach it. Padding on silent paws, she came back around to the cage door, sniffed again, and warily stepped inside.

'Slowly,' murmured Josie, as Emily got ready to spring. 'We don't want to scare her.'

Emily inched her way to the door of the cage and, holding her breath, afraid Lotta would leap out again, eased the door closed. Only when she heard the click of the catch did she relax.

Josie threw an old curtain over the cage. 'She should be calmer if it's dark,' she said. 'Besides, we don't want anyone to see inside, do we?'

Emily nodded, unable to speak. She felt all wobbly. She didn't have to worry any more. It was over.

She crouched beside the cage and wrapped her arms around it.

'Careful,' Josie warned. 'Those claws could easily slash through that curtain.'

But Emily didn't care. 'I'm sorry, Lotta,' she whispered. Sorry for what? For keeping her, or for letting her go? She didn't know. 'Sorry that I couldn't make it right for you.'

Josie crouched beside her. 'Lotta's a lot like you, isn't she?' she said.

Emily said nothing, just squeezed the cage tighter as though she could press all her love and longing into Lotta before she let her go.

'There are some things that can never be made right,' Josie said, softly, 'but I've found that when life takes something away, it also gives something new.'

'It's not the same.' Emily's voice was croaky.

'No. Not the same. Definitely different. But that doesn't mean it can't still be something good.'

Josie's shoulder, squirrel-grey and soft, looked so inviting. Emily let her head fall at last, and cried everything out into the warm fur.

20

Emily and Josie struggled to load the cage into the back of the car. To make things even more difficult, Lotta kept moving from one side to the other, so the cage was suddenly heavy at one end and then at the other. The spitting and growling brought Dad and Rufus outside to see what was going on. Dad was freshly shaved and looked so much more like his old self that Emily felt a rush of relief. Perhaps he was coming back from wherever he'd been inside his head.

Josie slammed shut the boot of her car with the cage inside. It was such a tiny car that the cage only just fitted, even with the back seats laid down flat.

Emily and Josie pressed themselves against the back of the car, side by side.

'What's going on here, hmm?' said Rufus. 'That your sister's dog in there? Hope it's going back where it belongs.'

'Oh yes, it *is*,' said Emily, earnestly. 'Dad, can I go with Josie to take it home?'

'That depends,' said Dad. 'Where does your sister live, Josie? Is it far? I don't want Emily to be a burden to you, and she does get terribly carsick.'

Emily looked at Josie. What would she say? They only needed to go half a mile down the road and let Lotta go, but they couldn't say that to Dad, could they?

'Cragforth,' blurted Josie. 'It's half an hour away, but she might ask us to stay for tea and cake, so we could be away all afternoon. If that's all right?'

A look of weary relief flickered across Dad's face before he managed to hide it. He must be pleased that Emily was going – glad to have her out of the way. So glad that he hadn't even realised she would have to sit in the front seat of the car. He always said it was safer in the back.

Josie's hand came down on Emily's shoulder, light but firm. 'We'll have some girly time together.'

Girly time with Josie? No way. Girly time was Friday evenings with a DVD and popcorn, in fluffy dressing gowns; it was going to the shops to look for some sparkly shoes to wear to Aunty Jill's wedding, then hot chocolate at the café afterwards. It was having a mini sleepover in Mum's bed when Dad was away on a night call and the wind was howling around the drainpipes outside while she nestled close to Mum's soft warmth and drifted to sleep to the sound of her breathing.

Girly time belonged to her and Mum. Nobody else.

'Maybe I'll just stay at home,' she began, looking pleadingly at Dad and willing him to agree. 'I would have to sit in the front and you won't let me.'

'I'm sure you'll be perfectly safe. A minute ago, you were all keen to go with Josie,' said Dad, 'and now you don't want to. You can't keep changing your mind. Are you going or staying?'

All three of them were staring at her. The tiny car shuddered at Emily's back. Lotta must be bouncing around in there, going half-crazy beneath the flowered curtain. What would she think if Emily didn't go with her back to the forest? She would feel abandoned, that Emily didn't love her.

'All right, I'll go,' she said in a small voice.

She got in the car with Josie, and the engine spluttered into life. In the back, Lotta yowled.

'She doesn't like the cold,' explained Josie.

'But she's used to it. She'd better be, if she's going to live back in the forest.'

Josie smiled. 'I meant the car.' She laid her arm along the back of Emily's seat and looked behind, ready to reverse. 'We don't want to run over Rufus now, do we?' she said, with a wink.

There was so much snow the little car could barely get out of the gate. Dad and Rufus had to throw their weight against the back and push, while Emily prayed that the flowery curtain wouldn't slip and reveal a certain furry surprise. The thought of their faces if that happened brought a tiny smile to her face.

'That's better,' said Josie, once they were on the road. 'Look, we've got the afternoon to ourselves. How about we see Lotta safely home and then go and find somewhere nice to have afternoon tea? The main road will be clear.'

Perhaps it wouldn't be so bad after all. As long as Josie didn't call it *girly time* again. They could just be two friends having a snack together. That was all. Mum wouldn't mind.

It was a slow journey, the little car skidding and sliding all over the place. At one point, they nearly went into the ditch and Emily had to cling to the dashboard so hard her knuckles turned white.

'Here?' said Josie.

'Just a bit further.' Emily pointed to the spot where she had found Lotta with her dead mother. Thank goodness the blood stain would be buried beneath the snow. But would Lotta remember? Would it upset her to come back here?

Josie stopped the car and the two of them went round to the back.

'She's too heavy for us to lift her out in the cage and carry it through the trees,' said Josie. 'We'll have to open it up here and let her jump out in her own time.'

'But what if someone comes?' said Emily.

Josie looked up and down the lane. 'Nobody would be idiot enough to drive down here without a good reason. And if anyone did come, and they saw something, it would be their word against ours. I would just say we stopped to let the dog out to stretch its legs, and that they were mistaken. Glare of the snow, the shadows in the forest. We could spin a pretty convincing tale, I'm sure.' She opened the boot. 'Ready?'

'No. Wait.' Emily tugged at the flowery curtain and it slithered off the cage. Lotta sat there, hunched in on herself. 'I don't think I can let her go.'

The reassuring weight of Josie's arm rested on Emily's shoulders.

'Why not?'

'Because ... because she might get scared, out there in the woods on her own. She might think her mum is still there, and she'll be searching and searching…' Emily blinked hard. 'She won't *know*. She won't understand.'

'Remember she's a wild animal,' said Josie. 'Life is very different for them. They accept death in a way that we … well, we struggle with.' She let her head rest against Emily's for a moment. 'And she won't be alone. There are other lynx out here, too.'

Emily nodded vigorously. 'I know that, and I know she should be out here where she belongs, but it's just…'

Josie waited. Lotta gave a grumbly yowl as if to say, *Get on with it!*

'Just…?' said Josie gently.

'Just that she's my friend – maybe my only friend here now that Dibs…' Emily's voice trailed off. 'I … I'll miss her, that's all.' Her arm crept around Josie's waist.

'Missing someone is hard,' said Josie, 'but it means that you loved them very much. And, usually, that they loved you very much too. Nobody can ever take that away from you.'

'Do you think Lotta loves me?' asked Emily.

'It's hard to say. I don't think a wild animal can love you the same as a pet can. But you did a very kind thing for Lotta, and now it's time to let her go free.'

Emily took a deep breath, held it for a moment, then released it, the vapour curling into the cold air.

'It's okay, Lotta,' she said. 'If you do get scared, remember I'll still be here for you. If you need me, you just come and find me, okay?'

She released the catch, opened the door, then stood back.

'Now watch what she does,' murmured Josie.

Lotta got to her feet and half crouched, half stood at the entrance of the cage. She sniffed the air and her dark pupils shrank to slits against the glare of the snow, making her eyes seem bigger and more golden than ever.

She jumped down, paws sinking up to her elbows in the snow.

'Goodbye, Lotta,' whispered Emily.

Lotta turned her head slowly and blinked. Then, with one bound, she was over the ditch and running, running into the trees, her dappled fur melting into the shadows and the spots of dark and light that rippled among the undergrowth.

Emily felt all shaky. She leaned against the side of the car and said, 'What now?'

'Hot chocolate,' said Josie. 'Definitely.'

'Not hot chocolate,' said Emily. 'That's Mum's drink. But,' she added hastily as Josie's face fell, 'something else instead.'

Josie nodded. 'It's a deal.'

Josie was right; the main road was clear of snow. Specks of grit flew up and smacked against the windscreen.

'Where are we going?' asked Emily.

'I know the perfect place,' said Josie, 'but do you mind if I just do something quickly first?'

'What is it?'

'Look in the glove compartment.' Josie nodded towards it. 'You'll find a Christmas present. It's for my mum.'

Emily pulled out a narrow package, wrapped in plain brown paper with spiky holly leaves stamped on it.

'I won't stay long,' said Josie. 'My mum lives in a care home. She isn't very well and doesn't recognise me any more. I'll just call in and give her the present, then we'll be on our way.'

Emily's hand shot to her mouth as she remembered something. 'I need to get a Christmas present for Dad,' she said, 'but I don't have any money.'

'I could help you to make something. What does he like?'

Emily tried to think. He used to play cricket every summer, but he gave up when Mum died. He liked action movies but he had to wait until Emily had gone to bed to watch them and said it was no fun on his own anyway, so he never bothered any more.

'I don't know,' she said.

'Okay then, what does he *love*?'

'That's easy,' said Emily. 'Mum.' She thought a bit more. 'And me. And Grandma Underwood, I think.'

'Favourite colour?'

'Green. Not bright green, but dark, like the forest.'

'I'll give it some thought,' said Josie.

After about ten minutes, they turned in at the gate of a big old house, gravel crunching beneath a thin layer of snow. A holly wreath with a scarlet ribbon hung on the door. Josie looked straight ahead, her hands gripping the steering wheel.

'Do you want to stay here? Or would you like to come in?'

Emily looked at the tall, forbidding building. It looked a bit spooky, despite the warm glow in the windows. But the thought of sitting out here on her own was worse.

'I'll come in,' she said.

Inside, the rooms smelled like cough medicine mixed with a bit of wee. Radiators pumped out waves of heat and Emily had to unzip her coat. Josie signed her name in a big book and a bored-looking girl in a blue uniform waved them through a door that swung both ways.

Josie tapped at a pink-painted door that said *Irene* on it. Nobody answered, but Josie went in anyway. Emily followed her in.

A tiny woman sat in high-backed chair by the window, her back hunched. Her mouth hung slackly open, but when she saw them, she smiled as though it was Christmas morning.

'You've come at last!' she said, clapping her hands together. 'Oh, my Josie, I've been waiting so long to see you.'

Josie's mouth fell open in surprise, but it was Emily the old lady reached out her hands to.

'*I'm* Josie, Mum,' said Josie, stepping forward and laying a hand on her mother's shoulder. 'This is my friend, Emily.' She beckoned Emily over and whispered, 'She thinks you're me, that I'm still a little girl. Here. You'd better give her this.' She handed over the present.

Nervously, Emily went to the old lady and handed

her the wrapped parcel. Two scrawny arms came around her neck. 'Thank you, my darling,' the old lady croaked. 'I've missed you so much.'

Back in the car, Josie was quiet and thoughtful. 'I think you just made my mum's day,' she said, 'but it's been a long one for me. Do you mind if we just go home?'

'We have hot chocolate,' said Emily solemnly, 'but no electricity.'

'Hot chocolate?' said Josie. 'Are you sure?'

Emily thought for a moment, and then she nodded.

Josie burst into a funny, snorty, wet laugh and pulled her into a hug.

🐾

It was quite exciting having no power in the cottage that night. Dad lit the fire, and the leaping glow flickered against the walls. They had a cold supper of cheese sandwiches and crisps, which meant that Dad never asked about the chicken that was missing from the fridge. Emily thought she could probably live on cheese for quite a while – even for Christmas dinner – if it meant she could avoid answering questions about the meat mystery.

Dad had used the gas cooker to heat up some water so he could wash the panda blanket. He hadn't done a great job – it was still a bit smelly and, as it steamed gently in the heat from the fire, the smell reminded Emily of the old people's home.

'No TV, I'm afraid.' Dad flicked on the battery-powered radio and the sound of some choirboys singing Christmas carols filled the room. 'Did you have a nice time with Josie? You were away a long time.'

Emily thought about it. She *had* sort of had a nice time, she realised now. She and Josie had gone into the studio when they got back, and Josie had helped her to stick beads and stars and tiny pieces of smooth, green glass on to an old wooden photo frame. Then she had taken a photo of Emily and they had put it into the frame. It looked like something off a proper Christmas gift website, and Emily had hidden it under her pillow. Dad would love it, she was sure.

But she couldn't tell Dad about that or about letting Lotta go, could she? To avoid answering his question, she got up from her place on the saggy sofa and picked up the basket of Christmas decorations. Even heaped in a tangled pile, they caught the firelight and sparkled as though there was a living fire inside them.

'Christmas Eve tomorrow,' she said. 'May as well decorate the tree.'

Dad stared at her, mouth open. Then he snapped it shut and jumped up from the armchair. 'Of course. Yes. Great idea.' He hovered by the tree and flicked one of the branches. A shower of needles fell on to the floor. 'Do you want to … um … do it yourself?' His hands flapped in the air. 'Or would you like me to help you?'

Emily looked at Dad. She looked at the decorations. He would probably try and tell her where to put them and they would have an argument, and he wouldn't know how it should look anyway. But…

Her fingers curled around the edges of the basket.

'Let's do it together,' she said.

21

The cold woke Emily the next morning. Dad refused to let her sleep in the cupboard any more, because he liked to check that she was still there if he woke up in the night. Her panda blanket was still slightly damp, and her other covers had slipped off to one side. There was no heating – without electricity, the boiler wouldn't work, and the radiators wouldn't come on.

Emily rolled over to look at her clock before she remembered it wasn't there. She missed its comforting glow and a sudden pang of worry sent her stomach into a flutter. Whoever had the clock knew Emily's secret. The question was: would they tell the police?

Trying to shut out the thought, she hauled her covers back on and wriggled about a bit until she was quite cosy, lying there in the early morning dark, with only the glow of the star hanging in the window. She opened the curtains a bit so that anyone outside would be able to see it and know where to come.

Just in case.

As she was lying there, letting thoughts drift in and out, she remembered.

It was Christmas Eve.

Despite everything, she couldn't help a stab of excitement, but it quickly faded, leaving her hollow inside. Normally, Christmas Eve was the start of proper Christmas. Quite a lot of the time it was *better* than Christmas Day because there was still everything to look forward to. Mum would roll up her sleeves and get out the mixing bowls, and soon the kitchen would be filled with delicious baking smells: mince pies, a soft, spongy pudding for those who didn't like Christmas pudding (which was everyone except Nana Godwin, who liked it with a good dose of brandy), and the chocolatiest Yule log ever, rolled up while it was warm and then unrolled and filled with chocolate buttercream. Emily always put the finishing touches to it – a dusting of icing-sugar snow and a fat robin.

Emily blinked quickly. There would be none of that this year.

None of anything. No Mum. No baking. No Nana

Godwin. And what about presents? Had Dad even thought of that?

Her bed wasn't comfy any more, and the star was stupid, swinging around up there all by itself. Who was going to see it? A big, fat nobody, that was who.

🐾

The morning dragged by like a miserable snail. Emily wanted to watch TV but there was still no power. She couldn't even play a game on her tablet because it was out of charge, and so was Dad's phone.

The Christmas tree, which had looked halfway to magical last night, was an overdressed twig this morning, and Emily couldn't find a thing right with it.

'What are we having for Christmas dinner tomorrow?' she asked, hoping that Dad wouldn't say *chicken*.

'Unless the power comes on, sandwiches again.' Dad was in a foul mood as well. 'For goodness' sake, go outside or something.'

'I thought I wasn't allowed to go out on my own.' Emily scraped at the threadbare velvet on the arm of the sofa until a hole appeared. 'You'll have to come with me.'

'I can't. I've got things to sort out.'

Despite herself, a smile popped on to Emily's face. 'Things?' Did he mean presents?

'I might have to go out later. You'll be all right by yourself for an hour or two, won't you?' He raised his eyebrows. 'See? I *do* know you're not a baby and that you're sensible enough to look after yourself. By the way, that kitten's turned up. The lynx.'

'Has it?' Emily put on her best innocent face. 'Do they know where it's been?'

'No idea. But Andy and Granger spotted it in the forest this morning, seemingly none the worse for wear.' Dad rubbed his hand across his face. 'Probably whoever had it realised that looking after a wild animal is nothing like having a pet.'

So Granger knew where Lotta was. And if he had killed her mother, what might he do to Lotta?

'Will they look after it?' she said anxiously. 'The Link Slink people?'

Dad nodded. 'They'll make sure it's managing to find food. Probably get a tracking collar on it, too, so they know where it is. Andy's gone away for Christmas now, but I'm sure Granger will keep an eye on it.'

A sick feeling washed over Emily. 'But what if someone shoots her, like they shot her mother?'

'How do you know it's a girl?' laughed Dad. 'Don't worry, it'll be watched a lot more closely this time. They all will.'

'Where are you going?'

Dad looked at her blankly. 'What?'

'Later. You said you were going out later.'

He gave a faint smile. 'You're hard to follow sometimes, Em. You jump from one thing to another like a grasshopper.'

But he didn't answer her question.

🐾

It was a low, dreary kind of day. The snow lay thick on the ground but the sky pressed down so close, it was like being trapped in a room where the ceiling was coming down, lower and lower, to squash her.

After another cold lunch, she moped around the cottage, half-heartedly rummaging in corners and drawers in case Dad might have hidden anything there. It was hard to see in the dim light, but even with the help of her torch, she found nothing, which meant that either he had hidden her presents too well or...

Or he had forgotten.

'Em?'

She was peering under his bed when he shouted, and she jumped, banging her head on the bed frame.

'I have to go out.'

She wriggled out backwards and yelled back, 'Where are you going?'

'I should be back in a couple of hours. Josie said she'd be out, but you can pop over to the farm if you need anything.'

As if she would be welcome there now.

She ran to the top of the stairs. 'I said, where are you going?'

'See you later.'

The front door slammed. Emily ran to her bedroom and climbed on to the bed just in time to see Dad getting into the passenger seat of Rufus's Range Rover before it drove away. Where could they be going together? They couldn't stand each other, and Dad despised big, fuel-guzzling cars.

All very strange. She couldn't help but worry that it had something to do with Lotta. Then a thought struck her. Now was her chance – the moment she'd been waiting for. Rufus had gone out, which meant she might be able to get into his house. She could find out whether he used red gun cartridges. If he only had blue ones, then she would know that Granger was the lynx killer.

She rummaged in her underwear drawer and pulled out the red cartridge from inside the odd sock. Without waiting to think, in case she chickened out, she dressed quickly, thundered down the stairs and jumped off halfway down, landing on the sofa. She charged into the kitchen and pulled on her wellies. She would do this for Lotta. And for Lotta's mother.

Rufus's back door was unlocked. It opened into a large kitchen with a high ceiling. Melted snow dribbled from Emily's boots on to uneven, red-brown tiles. A brass tap drip-drip-dripped into a huge white sink with a crack down one side. Piled in the sink and to either side of it were dirty dishes. There were knives and forks with food dried on them, mugs with tea stains, and an old dishcloth over the edge of the sink that was dried and crispy when she picked it up.

It smelled cold. Abandoned.

She stopped dead. What about the person she'd heard crying? What if they were still here? Rufus hadn't mentioned any visitors, but that didn't mean there weren't any.

She would have to be quick. And quiet.

There weren't any gun cartridges to be seen, but he must keep them somewhere. Did he have a locked cabinet, like Sal did? He didn't need one, did he? He didn't have any children that could pick them up and play with them. His daughter was all grown up and gone away, only last week. That must be her in the silver-framed picture propped up on the kitchen table – which was an odd place to keep it, next to a single table mat covered in crumbs and an empty plate with a knife and fork across it. Perhaps he liked to look at it while he ate. The woman reminded Emily of a deer, her hair dark and her smile shy. Nothing like Rufus.

After a quick peek out of the window to make sure nobody was coming, Emily hurried to the door on the far side of the kitchen. It opened on to a dark hallway with a couple of doors and a staircase. There was no sign of a locked cabinet of any kind; only a table with spindly legs and an old-fashioned landline telephone. Emily was about to try the first door when she heard something.

The throaty roar of a Range Rover, the slam of a car door and a voice: 'Jacky! Heel, you scoundrel.'

They were back. Rufus must have forgotten something.

The back door crashed open and claws skittered against the tiles. The only thing to do was to hurry up the stairs as fast as she could, which was difficult when she was also trying be quiet. Perhaps she could lie low until he went away.

At the top of the stairs, the landing turned sharply

right. There was a door to the left. She thought about the direction of Badger Cottage from here. The room behind that door must be back to back with Emily's own bedroom. Somehow, it felt safest to go in there, as though she might find a secret passageway that would lead her back home. She tiptoed in. The heavy door closed behind her with a *clunk* and she leaned against it, heart hammering.

Had Rufus heard? Perhaps not, but Jacky had – she could hear him barking frantically, until Rufus said something sharp and angry, and the racket stopped. She was safe. For now.

She looked around the room. Funny to think that her own bed was right there, just behind that wall, right where a double bed was pressed up against *this* side. This must have been where those strange noises came from – the wailing on that first night when she had seen the beast in the lane and then again later, when someone had definitely been crying. Rufus had said it was Jacky the first time, but she didn't believe him. What was he hiding?

Her hand tightened around the door knob. She didn't want to stay in here; it was creepy. But she couldn't go downstairs while Rufus was there.

Above the bed hung a large photograph, black and white, of a man and a woman. It looked like a wedding picture, judging by the flowers the woman was holding, although she didn't have a posh white dress, only a grey-looking jacket and skirt that could have been any colour at all. She had dark hair, half-hidden by a small hat with a veil on it. She looked like the young woman in the photo downstairs.

One side of the bed was neatly made, the pillow clean and smooth; the other side was rumpled, the greasy-looking pillow dinted with the shape of a head. It was a bed for two, with only one person sleeping in it.

Bedside cabinets stood on both sides, one messy and the other neat and tidy. On the messy one was a water glass with stale bubbles in it and a book called *Growing through Grief*. On the neat one stood a small lamp, a square alarm clock and a lace-edged handkerchief. The clock was so similar to Emily's that she went over and picked it up, but no – it was smaller, and it had stopped. There was no comforting *whirr* as the batteries drove the hands round and round. The hands said twenty-five past ten.

She picked up the handkerchief and sniffed it. It smelled like the soap Nana Godwin had in her bathroom. And suddenly she missed Nana so much that it was like a fist in her stomach, twisting. Roses, that was it. It smelled of roses.

There was a rush of air around her and the door juddered in its frame. Another door slammed downstairs.

It's all right, she told herself, *it's Rufus going out again.*

But her stomach kept twisting and suddenly the face of the young man smiling out of the wedding picture and the fading scent of the hanky reminded her that people lost other people all the time and there was nothing – nothing at all – they could do to bring them back. In a rush of dizziness, she felt as though *she* was the one in danger of being lost.

Forgetting all about being quiet, or looking for gun cartridges, she yanked open the door, charged down the stairs and raced back into the kitchen. She didn't care if Rufus found her, or Dad, or anyone. She *wanted* someone to discover her, just so she could be with them, however furious they might be. Because if she was with someone – anyone – then maybe she might not feel so hollow, as if she had the delicate bones of a bird.

She ran across to the studio, hoping that Josie would be back. But the door was locked and no matter how much she rattled the knob, it wouldn't open. So much for people not leaving their doors locked around here.

There was nothing for it but to go back to Badger Cottage and wait for Dad to come back. She burst in through the back door and hurried into the living room. Everything seemed too quiet. She looked around, panting, but there was no reassuring hum of hot water in the radiators. There was no clanking and clattering of pans in the kitchen. No television, no fridge humming and groaning in the kitchen. Even the birds outside had gone quiet.

She stood in the middle of the lounge, perfectly still, listening to the sound of the cottage creaking and settling around her, and a prickly patter as another bundle of needles fell off the Christmas tree.

So this was what lonely really felt like.

All that time, when she'd been scared of the lynx stalking the darkness, this was what she had really been afraid of. Not something out there – not even something inside the cottage – but inside *Emily*. Where she couldn't get away from it.

Josie wasn't in. Dad and Rufus had gone on some mysterious mission and Dibs didn't want anything to do with her – he had made that clear when he had threatened to shoot her. And people didn't say that kind of thing to people they wanted to stay friends with, not even as a joke.

There was only one person she could think of

nearby that might be pleased to see her. Well, not a *person*, exactly.

'Lotta,' whispered Emily.

22

She ran blindly, head down, out of the front door and into the lane, then along the road that led to the forest. She didn't want to go *into* the forest, not with the adult lynx prowling about in there, but perhaps she could catch a glimpse of Lotta between the tree trunks.

The sky was the colour of cold porridge, darkening at the edges. It was only three in the afternoon, but dusk wasn't far away. Glad of her gloves and thick woolly hat, Emily trudged through the snow until she reached the bit where the field ended and the forest began. Instead of continuing along the road, she climbed through the wooden fence – which was honestly a bit broken *before* she put her foot on it – and stepped into the field.

Looking right, the land sloped gently down towards Dibs's farm. Looking left, the forest was thick and dark, like a troop of soldiers waiting for the command to advance on the farm and attack it. Emily raised her arm, ready to give the order. That would teach him to be so horrid to her.

On the other side of the field, the trees curved round and the forest went down to meet the narrow, grassy track where Flump had nearly got squashed by Granger's car. Emily decided that she would walk along the edge of the trees, right down to the lane. That way, she could check for paw prints in the snow and see if Lotta had come out into the field at all.

She felt a bit better now, with something to do. But the dreadful ache of loneliness was still there, inside her head, inside her chest. She felt as though it might eat her from the inside out unless she kept moving. Looking alternately at the snow and at the trees beside her, Emily made her way along the edge of the forest down the hill towards the lane.

She stopped, studying some paw prints that came diagonally up the field and disappeared into the trees. They were about the right size for Lotta, but they had claw marks. Probably a fox or a dog.

A sudden shiver went through her. What if this was the dog that had attacked the sheep? It might be lurking among the trees right now, watching her, its jaws glistening with saliva as it waited for the right moment to pounce…

Emily ran.

She kept going until she was almost at the grassy track, where she slowed down. There were some different prints here – ones she couldn't figure out. Next to a large hole in the hedge, the snow was flattened and scuffed about, then there were a few small prints that could have been from a child or a deer, or something else. It was hard to tell because the prints sank deep into the snow and she couldn't see what the shape was at the bottom. Which meant they could also be from a lynx. Every metre or two, the same scuffled patch appeared again. It was like some kind of code – *dot, dot, splat; dot, dot, splat*. Stranger still was the faint smear of red in every scuffled patch.

It looked horribly like blood.

The tracks crossed the corner of the field and disappeared into the trees. Emily glanced up anxiously. It was beginning to get properly dark now, an inky stain bleeding into the sky and a curved half-moon clawing the tops of the trees. What should she do? Should she go into the forest and try to follow the tracks? Or should she just forget all about it? She was so tired of trying to do the right thing. She didn't know what the right thing was any more.

Shouts drifted down the lane from the farm. Not the everyday shouts of Dibs calling to Streak and yelling at the sheep, but something higher, shriller, with a panicky edge.

'Flump? Flump! Where are you? Come on, it's not a game.' That was definitely Dibs.

'Flump, sweetheart! Mummy's here. Come on, it's time to come indoors. Flump!' That was Sal, her voice swooping and dipping like a wounded bird.

Footsteps down the lane. 'Flump?'

'Dibs?'

He jumped, swore under his breath. 'Soup, is that you? What are you doing lurking behind the hedge? Is Flump with you?'

'No.' Emily looked at the tracks, and she looked at the hole in the hedge. Dibs, on the other side, lifted his torch, blinding her for an instant. 'But I think he might have been this way.'

Dibs wasted no time in dropping to his hands and knees and crawling through the hole. 'Need to fix that,' he muttered. 'Always something for me to…' His voice sputtered to a halt as he took in the strange prints. 'Step, step, fall over,' he murmured to himself. 'That's Flump, all right.' His face suddenly paled in the torchlight. 'Is that *blood*?'

'I think so,' said Emily, in a ghost of a voice. 'Did he hurt himself?'

'I don't know!' Dibs's voice had gone all strange

and squeaky. 'I thought Mum was watching him and she thought I was. He's a right beggar for running off on his own.'

He crouched, pressing his hand against the red smear on the snow. 'Soup, the lynx that attacked the sheep … what if it gets Flump too? He's about the same size, maybe smaller. He'd be an easy target.'

'You don't know it was a lynx.' Emily's voice was colder than the wind that was tugging at her hair and sliding its icy fingers beneath her hood.

'And *you* don't know that it *wasn't*.' Dibs glared at her. 'Either way, I'm going to get some help. My baby brother's out there on his own, he's hurt and it's going dark. And it's well below freezing. If the lynx doesn't get him, he'll probably get hypothermia. And all you care about is those stupid cats.'

'That's not true!' Of course she cared about them, but she cared about Flump, too. She pictured him tottering through the trees, curls bobbing, crying for Sal and getting all snotty and afraid, and falling over. 'I'll help you look for him. Have you got another torch?'

'Forget it,' snarled Dibs. 'We don't need your help.'

He wriggled back through the hole and jogged away, back towards the farm, the torchlight raking the snow as he went.

Emily was shaking with rage and fear. There was still just enough light to see by, so she did the only thing she could. Let Dad worry if he came back; this was more important.

She stepped into the forest.

Everything sounded different in here. There were lots of tiny cracks and scuffles, creaks and the soft moan of the wind in the treetops. There were other lynx here. Not just Lotta, but the bigger ones. The ones that could bring down a deer. For the first time, doubt pricked at the edge of her mind. Could a lynx have attacked the sheep?

The thought made her want to turn and run, out of the trees, away from Littendale altogether. But she kept on going, step by step, following Flump's tracks. He seemed to be wandering about, twisting from one direction to another, in and out of the trees.

'Flump?' called Emily. She stopped walking and listened for a cry, a wail, a yell. But she couldn't hear anything.

A good twenty minutes must have passed before she heard something in the distance. A murmur of voices. On a clear night like this, sound could carry for miles, but something about it made her nervous.

She kept on walking and calling; walking, calling and listening.

She stopped, the sound of her own breathing noisy in her ears. A small blue mitten lay in the snow, ripped and bloodstained at one end. There was the familiar flattening of the snow where Flump must have fallen over, and the streak of red. It must be his hand that was bleeding.

But, in the pale light of the rising moon, she saw something else. Paw prints, coming out of the trees and circling around the bloody spot. Paw prints where something had sniffed at that blood. Paw prints without claws, which had followed Flump through the trees, tracking him closely, as the hunter tracks his prey.

23

The murmur in the distance was louder now, and closer. It was definitely people – quite a big group, by the sound of it. Dibs must have managed to round up quite a search team. Emily kept walking until she reached a rocky outcrop in a clearing. Breaking twigs and rustling undergrowth made it difficult to listen for anything else. The mob of people burst out of the trees.

She shrank back, away from the lights and the rough voices, but she'd already been spotted. There was a shout, and Dibs came running towards her.

'I thought I told you to keep out of this.'

'I'm not leaving a little kid on his own in the dark,' she snapped. She caught the glint of moonlight on metal. 'They've brought *guns*?' she gasped. 'What for?'

'What do you think?' said Dibs. His gaze fell on the blue mitten in Emily's hand. He snatched it from her and made a weird gulping noise. 'Do you know which way he went?'

Emily wished for time to stretch itself out so that she could think about her answer. If she said no, Flump might be in danger; if she said yes, then the mob would trail the lynx and probably kill it. And she didn't *actually* know which way Flump had gone; only which way he had come.

'You do, don't you?' Dibs bared his teeth, almost wild himself. 'Tell me.'

Despite meaning not to look, Emily's eyes flicked down to the tracks on the ground. Dibs looked too. 'Lynx,' he spat, 'and dog too.'

Emily looked more closely. She hadn't noticed that – clawed prints weaving in and out of the others. Did that mean Flump was being hunted by two predators? Her throat felt tight.

Dibs smiled, but not in a friendly way.

'Thanks,' he said, 'for nothing.'

Then he was away, trotting through the snow, waving the mitten and calling to the men and women who stood, shuffling and puffing out clouds of breath. Emily couldn't hear what he said when he reached them, but a roar went up. The people spread out in a wide line, beating the undergrowth and calling to one another.

Only Emily heard the panting in the trees over to her right, the sound of something moving, of claws scrabbling against rock.

All she could think of now was Flump. 'Over here!' she yelled. A wave of sound rose and fell, and footsteps came crashing towards her.

'What? What is it?' It was the butcher from the village, his huge hands cradling a shotgun. Close behind him was Granger, his face shadowed by the peaked hood of his waterproof coat.

'Have you found him?' Sal pushed her way through to the front, her eyes deep pools in her face.

Emily shook her head. 'Listen,' she said.

They all listened. 'Can't hear anything,' rumbled the butcher.

'She's probably trying to put us off the scent,' said Dibs. 'Just ignore her.'

'I'm not!'

The crowd grumbled and growled at her, and moved away, fanning out into a long line again.

Emily turned the other way. Only Emily noticed the tracks, zig-zagging through the trees. Only Emily took all the courage she could summon, gritted her teeth, and followed them into the dark.

She wished she'd brought a torch with her. Tree roots tripped her and brambles snatched at her coat, ripping and tearing. By the sound of it, the mob was coming closer again, moving round in a big circle. At some point they would meet head on.

Stumbling into another, smaller clearing, she saw them. Curled against a tree trunk was a lynx. Not any lynx, but her very own Lotta, hissing at her sudden approach.

And right next to her, lying in the snow, fast asleep, was Flump.

Emily kept her distance, uncertain what to do. She could see from here that Flump's hand was bleeding quite badly. Was he asleep, or was he unconscious? Either way, it was clear that Lotta wasn't there to harm him.

Emily laughed out loud with relief, which made Flump startle. So he was only sleeping, and Lotta – whether she knew it or not – was keeping him *warm*. Emily knew that a wild animal wouldn't really think to help a human like that, but Lotta's kitten instinct to move close to a source of warmth had probably saved his life on this deadly cold night.

She barely had time to register this before the mob crept out of the trees opposite, melting in and out of the shadows in ones and twos. They'd seen Lotta and Flump too.

And five guns were pointing directly at them.

24

'I told you!' Dibs called across the clearing. 'First that lynx killed our sheep and now it's bitten my baby brother as well.'

'That lynx,' Emily shouted back, 'did *not* kill your sheep, and I know that for a fact.'

'Oh yeah? How do you know, lynx lover? Were you there?'

Sal stepped forwards, Nessie and Bean right behind her. 'I'm going to get my son,' she announced. She moved towards Lotta, who stood up and snarled. Flump stirred, woke and began to whimper. 'It's all right, sweetheart,' Sal said. 'Mummy's here.'

Dibs put an arm in front of Sal, even though she was twice his size. 'I'll get him. It might be dangerous.'

'No, I'll do it,' said Emily. 'You'll only scare her.'

She walked into the middle of the clearing. Some of the five men holding guns looked at her, as though they were wondering whether to shoot her instead.

'I said, *I'll* do it.' Dibs strode towards her until they stood, face to face and toe to toe. 'And what do you mean, you'll only scare *her*? How do you know it's a girl? Why are you so worried about the lynx when you can see what it's done to my brother?' His eyes held a challenge.

'Deek! Deek!' whimpered Flump. 'Deek bite!' He held his hand out towards Dibs.

'What's he saying?' asked Emily.

'He's telling us that the lynx bit him, stupid.' Dibs took a step towards Lotta and Flump; Emily matched his step.

She began to murmur to Lotta, crooning about the nasty old dark and whispering to her.

Lotta's ears, against her head until now, flickered towards Emily and their eyes met.

'It's all right,' said Emily, half speaking and half singing. 'Nobody's going to hurt you.'

Lotta seemed to relax a little. She walked a couple of steps away from Flump and sat down on a flat rock.

'How do you *do* that?' hissed Dibs. 'It's almost as though it *recognises* you.' He turned to Emily. 'Does it?'

She didn't answer that. 'Get Flump,' she said through gritted teeth, then continued to sing to Lotta.

Dibs didn't need to get Flump. The toddler got to his feet and tottered over, still whimpering, 'Deek! Deek bite!' and shaking his head sadly. His face was smeared with tears and snot, his hair matted and his clothes filthy and wet. 'Naughty deek. Naughty!' He threw himself into Dibs's open arms, and a sigh of relief went through the gathered crowd. Sal ran to hug them both.

The moment Flump was clear, the men all trained their guns on Lotta. Emily heard the click of safety catches being released. They were ready to shoot.

'No!' she yelled, and went to stand in front of Lotta.

'Get out of the way, you stupid girl,' a man shouted.

Behind her, Emily could sense Lotta slinking away, her paws silent in the snow.

'The wretched thing's going that way!' The guns swivelled to Emily's right. She sidestepped so that she was in front of them again.

'You're not shooting her. She's done nothing wrong.'

'If you won't shift, lass, then I'll shift you.' A short, stocky man wearing a flat cap lowered his gun and came striding towards Emily. Two black Labradors trotted behind him, in the shadows.

'You'll have to shift me and all.' Someone moved forward, hood pulled low over his face, and stood beside Emily.

'Granger, get out of there,' snarled the flat-cap man.

'You're not shooting the lynx,' said Granger.

Emily blinked in confusion. 'But you shot one,' she hissed.

'No, I didn't!' He pulled back his hood and turned to face her. 'I'm protecting them.'

'But I thought … the pheasants in your car…'

Granger folded his arms across his chest. 'I was telling the truth about them, all right? A lot of people think stuff about me. Doesn't mean they're right.'

So if it wasn't Granger, then it must be…

'I said, *move*.' The flat-cap man grabbed her arm and was trying to pull her aside when two more people came out of the trees.

'Get your hands off my daughter!' Dad was out of breath. Rufus followed more slowly behind him.

Rufus. The lynx killer.

Emily shrank away from him as he approached.

'She's causing trouble,' the flat-cap man growled at Dad.

'If you don't do as Underwood tells you, I'll cause trouble for *you*, hmm?' said Rufus. 'How would you like to begin the new year unemployed? What would your wife say then?'

The man touched his cap and retreated. 'Sorry, boss. Didn't see you there. Just trying to protect your birds.'

'Mr Underwood, could you look at my son's hand?' said Sal, her voice tight with anxiety. 'He's been bitten by that lynx and he's bleeding pretty badly.'

Emily willed Lotta to run, but she realised that a few people had separated from the mob and gone round behind the lynx. They were waiting in the trees, ready to block her path if she tried to escape. She prowled back and forth, ears flattened, growling to herself as though she was wondering what to do.

Flump pressed himself against Sal as Dad went over to him.

'Let's have a look at your hand, matey,' said Dad.

Flump shook his head and buried his face against Sal's leg. 'Deek bite,' he whimpered.

'He's trying to say *teeth*,' explained Sal. 'Yes, darling, the teeth did bite you, didn't they?'

She persuaded Flump to let Dad examine his hand. Dad shone a torch on it and peered closely at the wound. 'Doesn't look like a bite from a lynx,' he said, frowning. 'The teeth marks are all wrong. Whatever did this had a longer jaw. In fact, it looks more like a...'

The two Labradors suddenly began barking madly. Something brown and white slunk out of the trees, keeping low to the ground, tail pressed between its legs, lips peeled back to reveal yellowing teeth.

'Streak,' said Dibs. 'Where have you been, lass? What's wrong?'

'Deek!' Flump went crazy and tried to scramble up Sal's leg as though she was a tree trunk. 'Deek *bite*.'

'I think,' said Emily slowly, 'he's trying to say that *Streak* bit him.'

'No, no, Flump. It was the cat that bit you,' insisted Dibs.

'*Deek*.' Flump was screaming and crying now. Even though Sal had picked him up, he burrowed against her, feet digging into her ribs.

Lotta was pacing up and down behind Emily. Streak noticed her and snarled.

'Stay back, Streak,' warned Emily, holding her hand out to ward off the dog.

'Emily, come away,' said Dad wearily. 'You can't do any more now.' Emily saw that he had a gun too.

In an instant, Streak leapt at Emily's hand and bit down, hard. A flash of white-hot pain seared through her flesh and she could feel a strange tearing sensation. She screamed, trying to snatch her hand away, but Streak's jaw was clamped firmly around it.

'Get away, Streak!' It was Dibs, rushing towards them.

Streak let go and bounded towards Lotta instead. Emily, her hand released, staggered back and fell to the ground.

Dad lifted his gun and aimed it at Streak.

'No!' yelled Dibs.

Dad fired once, reloaded the gun and pointed it at Lotta.

Then he fired again.

25

Dad came running to Emily and knelt beside her in the snow. 'Keep your hand raised above your head,' he instructed. 'Do you feel faint?'

Emily tried to nod, but it came out as a weird shake of the head. Rufus calmly unfolded his special walking stick to reveal a seat, and shook out a clean white handkerchief. 'Need to sit down, hmm?' he said. 'Use this to bind up the wound if you like, Underwood.' He burrowed in his pocket and brought out a silver flask. 'And perhaps a nip of whisky, hmm? For the shock, you know.'

'She's too young,' said Dad, 'but I wouldn't mind a swig myself in a minute.' He bound Emily's hand with the handkerchief as she sat in the snow. She wasn't going to sit on the lynx killer's seat. 'If you feel woozy, get your head between your knees.'

Emily did feel decidedly woozy. How had

everything gone so wrong? Lotta, poor Lotta. Emily had let her down in every way possible. And her hand – she had never felt pain like it.

'Why did you have to kill them?' she managed to say. She was so dizzy she couldn't even focus to see the bodies.

'I didn't,' said Dad. 'I used tranquilliser darts. They're not dead; they'll just be knocked out while we sort out this mess.'

Emily squinted towards the trees. Sure enough, there was Lotta, prowling about, shaking her head as though something was stuck in her ear. After a couple of minutes she sat down, then swayed a bit, and finally rolled over onto her side. Dibs bent over Streak, who was laid out in the snow close to Emily.

'Why did he do that?' he was muttering. 'I can't believe he would do that.' He looked up at Dad, his eyes filled with fury. 'You shot my dog! I'll have the police on you for that!'

'She'll be awake in an hour or so.' Dad shuffled over on his bent knees. 'Is she always this aggressive?'

'She's always been a lovely dog,' snapped Sal. 'Very good-natured.'

'Not true,' mumbled Emily. Her head felt all fuzzy, and the voices around her seemed to be very distant. She let her head drop on to her knees and closed her eyes.

'Which is it?' demanded Dad.

'She's changed.' Dibs sounded as if the words were being dragged out of him. 'Used to be a real softie, but she's got ... I don't know. She's gone a bit off. Snapping at people, scared of sudden noises.'

Emily turned her head sideways, still resting it on her knees. 'Always hiding under the tractor.'

'Hmmm.' Dad pulled back Streak's lips to check the colour of her gums. 'What's this?' He tugged at something caught between Streak's teeth.

'What is it?' asked Dibs.

Without speaking, Dad showed Dibs what was in his hand.

'Wool.' Dibs's voice was flat. 'Sheep's wool.'

Emily blinked and sat up a bit. Her hand throbbed with every beat of her heart, but this was important. 'You mean it was *Streak* that killed the sheep?'

Dad shrugged. 'Looks like it.'

'But *why*?' Dibs choked.

'I think this dog has been poisoned.'

'*Poisoned*?'

Dad counted the symptoms on his fingers. 'Aggressive behaviour that's out of character; fear of sudden noises; hiding in dark places. And this.' He leant forward and wiped one finger along Streak's jaw. Emily could just see in the light of all the torches that it came away frothy. 'All symptoms of poisoning, probably lead.'

'But how? Where has it come from?' Sal stood over them with Flump virtually sitting on her head to keep as far away from Streak as possible.

Dad blew out a long breath through his nose. 'Could be anywhere on the farm. Lead pipes, old paint – especially red paint – or lead weights used in fishing.'

Emily struggled to string her thoughts together. They kept drifting apart. 'Did you say red paint? Dibs,' she said. 'Red paint! The old tractor!'

She remembered the flakes of red around Streak's muzzle as the dog dug in the soil beneath the tractor. Trying to hide from the thing that was upsetting her, and only making it worse.

'That old thing?' said Sal.

'You need to get rid of it,' said Dad. 'Make sure someone clears the place properly and safely so there's no trace left of the paint. And get him tested.' He nodded towards Flump. 'Where dogs show signs of lead poisoning, it's often found in small children too, even if they show no symptoms.'

Sal's mouth fell open. 'What about those two?' She pointed at Nessie and Bean, who were crouching near Streak, peering at her with open mouths.

'Them too.'

'What about Streak? Can you make her better?' The words felt like marbles rolling around in Emily's mouth.

Dad nodded, and Dibs sagged with relief. 'There's a treatment for it. Chelation, it's called. It mops up the lead from her blood. Hopefully it'll help her, get her back to her normal self.'

Some of the men had put their guns down. There was a lot of talk and bustle as they worked out how to carry Streak out of the forest.

'What about Lotta?' said Emily.

'Who?'

She was grateful that the dark hid her sudden fierce blush. How stupid to almost give the game away now!

'I...' she mumbled, swaying as she tried to stand.

Dad was at her side in a moment. 'Lean on me,' he said, and she did. It felt good. It felt safe. She heard the rasp of Dad's stubble against her coat as he spoke. 'We'll get the lynx and the dog back to the farm, where they can be penned in somewhere safe. Then we can have a good look at your hand and the little chap, too.' He nodded at Flump. 'You both might need some stitches.'

'The farm?' said Sal. 'I don't want that creature

anywhere near my animals. I've got lambing ewes to think about, and my kids.'

'Mum,' said Dibs, tugging at her sleeve. 'Look at it. It's not going to do any harm. It's only small.'

'I can probably get hold of a cage to put it in,' said Granger. Emily had almost forgotten he was there. 'That way you don't need to worry.'

Dad carried Emily out of the forest. 'You don't need to tell me now what you were doing there,' he said, 'but I would like to hear the whole story when you're feeling better.'

'The *whole* story?' asked Emily, seized with panic. Maybe it was *Dad* who had found her clock, and he was just waiting for the right moment to give her the roasting she deserved.

'But I just want you to know,' he said, 'that I'm very proud of you. And...' His voice broke a little and he tried to hide it by clearing his throat. 'And Mum would be too.'

26

The farmhouse seemed overcrowded with so many people crammed into it. All the family were there, plus Sal's sister, Alison, who had come to help with the search. Dad was talking on the phone, asking someone at the vet surgery to come and fetch Streak; she would stay there until the treatment for the lead poisoning began to work. Rufus stood in a corner looking awkward and taking little sips from his silver flask, and even Granger had been invited in for a warming cup of tea. He wrapped his hands gratefully around the steaming mug and eyed everyone warily.

Emily sat on her usual chair as a smiling on-duty doctor with bright-red lipstick and a jaunty ponytail checked her injury. She reminded Emily a tiny bit of Mum. The doctor crouched beside her to clean the wound with antiseptic wipes. It stung a lot but she managed not to pull away.

'Steri-Strips should do it,' said the doctor, as she laid the tiny, white, sticky strips across the bite, 'and some painkillers, but I'm afraid you'll need a tetanus jab, too.'

Dad finished his phone call at once and came over to hold Emily's hand as the needle went into her arm. 'That's my brave girl,' he said, dropping a kiss on her head.

Flump's wound was deeper and there was a flurry of activity as Sal got a bag of nappies and spare clothes ready to take him to the hospital for a check-up. She stopped beside Emily and rested a hand on her shoulder.

'Thank you,' she said. 'We might not have found him without you. You're welcome here any time.'

Dibs, who had been leaning against the wall looking ashamed of himself, slunk over.

'That's twice you've saved Flump now,' he said. 'Sorry I was mean to you, Soup. I was just ... well, I was worried, but I still shouldn't have shouted at you or said such horrible things.'

'It's okay,' said Emily, though it didn't feel okay, not yet. Her hand was actually hurting more now that the warmth of the kitchen was seeping through her body, and she couldn't stop thinking about Lotta, who was stretched out inside a cage in one of the calf pens on a bed of clean straw.

'What about the lynx?' she burst out.

'You don't need to worry about that any more,' said Dad. 'I spoke to Andy earlier. They're pulling the plug on the Lynx Link here. It's not really working out the way they hoped.'

'What?' Emily stood up, but her head felt all spinny so she sat down again. 'What will happen to her? To them, I mean.'

'They'll be taken back up to Scotland, where they came from. There's a lot more wild space there, and the rewilding has been a huge success. They won't disturb anyone, and no one will disturb them.'

'But...' Scotland was forever away. They had been there once on holiday, and it had taken a whole day of driving along twisty, turny roads. She felt sick at the thought. 'Can we go and visit?' she said in a small voice.

'We'll see.'

Emily knew what that meant. The same as it always meant when grown-ups said it: no.

'It's not fair,' she choked. 'Why should they be punished while the one who shot the lynx gets away with it?'

'We still don't know who it was,' admitted Dad.

'I do. It was *him.*' She pointed a wavering finger at Rufus. But somehow, she didn't feel angry any more.

She didn't want to get him into trouble, not now she knew how much he missed his wife and daughter.

'It wasn't Rufus,' sighed Sal. 'It was me.' A gasp rippled round the kitchen as she lifted Flump and held him close beneath her chin. 'I'm sorry. I shouldn't have done it. I thought our farm was in danger. I've got kids, you know? Young ones. And I'm on my own...'

'No, you're not.' Dibs stepped close and put his arm around her waist. She rested her cheek on the top of his head and Flump pulled at a chunk of his hair, making him yelp.

Emily folded her arms on the tabletop and let her head fall into them. She should be glad that everything was solved, though she didn't want Sal to be punished. She just felt numb. She would never see Lotta again.

'Come on,' said Dad gently. 'I have a surprise for you at ... back at the cottage.'

Home, he had been going to say *home*. But it wasn't. A surprise? He must have remembered to buy her a Christmas present after all. Emily snorted into her arms. So what? What did it matter? What did any of it matter any more?

She resisted at first, when he tried to prise her out of her hunched position. All she wanted was to go to bed and sleep forever. Or at least long enough to miss Christmas.

She felt a light touch on her shoulder. 'Soup? I know you're in there. Look, someone's here to see you.'

She opened her eyes to see Alexander nestled in Dibs's hands. Without speaking, she sat up and held out her arms. She hugged Alexander's adorable warmth to her chest and felt the tiniest rumble of his first purr against her ribs.

'I know how much you love cats of all kinds,' said Dibs, giving her a meaningful look, 'so why don't you have this one?'

'Really?'

'Why not? We've got too many cats around the place already.'

She turned to Dad. 'Can I? Oh, please say yes!'

Dad smiled. 'I don't see why not. Your responsibility though, if you're going to have a pet.'

Emily thought about how she'd tried to look after Lotta and how difficult it had all been on her own.

'Will you help me?' she said. 'Sometimes?'

'Of course,' said Dad, giving her a wink, 'although I don't think you'll need it. And now we need to be getting back.' He began to gather coats and wellies, to say goodbye to everyone. He looked like the old Dad again, bustling about being kind and helpful.

'Soup?' muttered Dibs.

She met his gaze. He was staring at her solemnly, holding out a small package wrapped clumsily in dark-blue paper with stars on it. 'Open it when you get home,' he said. 'Friends?'

Friends didn't turn against you when you needed them most. And that worked both ways. He'd been so worried about the farm and she hadn't even really noticed. She nodded.

'Friends.'

Rufus carried her home. When she tried to stand up, she found that she was still quite faint, and he caught her as she fell. He was surprisingly strong for an old man, and he sang something under his breath as they walked – some old-fashioned love song, by the sound of it. Emily wondered what it was really like for him, living alone in the house next door with only Jacky for company.

And suddenly, she understood: Rufus, Josie, Dad. Maybe even Sal, worrying about her husband and her family. And Granger, with everyone believing things about him that weren't true. Everyone was lonely in their own way.

By the time they got close to the cottage, Rufus was puffing and panting so much that Emily feared he might have a heart attack.

'I think I might be able to walk the last bit,' she said.

When she slithered off his back, her legs felt weak and spindly like a newborn lamb. But Dad offered his arm for her to hook hers through. Alexander was tucked safely inside his coat. Together, they walked back to the cluster of buildings that was Badger Cottage, the house and the courtyard, with Josie's studio tucked in behind.

Instead of going in the back way, they went to the front door. Something was different. It took Emily a few moments to work out what it was. Light was pouring from the windows, both upstairs and down. The power cut was over!

'Rufus and I went to fetch a generator and some oil,' explained Dad. 'We'll have light and heat now to see us through till the snow melts.'

'And you can have Christmas dinner, hmm?' added Rufus, still a touch wheezy from carrying her.

'Will you come too?' said Emily.

Rufus harrumphed and coughed. 'Well, I don't want to intrude...'

'That's a great idea!' Dad clapped him on the back. 'As long as you can put up with my cooking.'

Emily looked again at the window. Inside, she could see Josie moving about in the living room, adding a string of lights to the battered old Christmas tree. And several lengths of tinsel, which hid the bareness of the branches. Funny, that – she had managed to find some that looked just like the special tinsel Nana Godwin always used, with fluffy strands of gold and silver twined together.

It looked so cosy and welcoming, like a scene from a Christmas card.

And then there was the sound of feet coming slowly down the stairs just inside. The front door swung open, and there stood the last person Emily expected to see.

Nana Godwin.

27

The sweet, flaky pastry on the mince pies melted like a snowflake on Emily's tongue.

'Christmas Day,' she said. 'It never turns out quite how I expect it.'

'How do you mean?' asked Dad.

'Usually I'm really excited for weeks and on the actual day it turns out to be a bit … well, a bit *boring* by the afternoon; this year, I wasn't looking forward to it at *all* and it's turned out to be pretty good in the end.'

'I'm glad,' said Dad, 'and I love the photo frame.'

He had put it on the mantelpiece and brought down his wedding photo to stand alongside it so that Mum could join in with the celebrations. She smiled out at them all as if she thoroughly approved of everything.

Dad had given Emily a year's pass to the local zoo so she could go as many times as she liked, and Josie had given her a small painting of a lynx. Nana had brought herself, which was the best present Emily could ever have asked for.

'Nana,' she sighed, wriggling her toes with pleasure in front of the blazing fire, 'tell me again how you managed to get here.' Last night she had been so exhausted that she had been packed off to bed with hugs – and more than a few tears – all round.

'Well, I took that train after all,' said Nana. 'They told me at the station not to begin my journey, and that all trains were stopping in Rincastle, but I got on anyway.'

'So you got to Rincastle and…?'

'Then I had to take a bus, which took forever. The road was so slippery that they cancelled all the later buses – I got on the very last one. And then it broke down in the middle of nowhere with only me and a couple of young people on it…'

Emily smiled. *Young people.* That probably meant they were about fifty.

'…and a taxi driver came out to pick us up and managed to get us to Cragforth. Then I got completely stuck.'

Dad took up the story. '…which is where Rufus

and I picked her up in the Range Rover. It wasn't only the generator we went for, you know!'

Rufus was coming later for Christmas dinner; he was expecting a call from his daughter first. Emily had seen him out in the lane with Jacky this morning, a new tartan collar around the little dog's neck.

'What do you think of the Christmas tree?' said Josie with a smile. 'Your nana brought a bag of decorations with her from home. She tells me that it's not Christmas without them.'

'That's what *I* said,' agreed Emily. But there was something missing. 'Wait here. I just have to get something.'

She went upstairs a bit more slowly than usual. Her legs still felt a bit wobbly and her hand ached. Dad had bandaged it properly and she rather liked it. It looked impressive.

The star was still hanging in her bedroom window, twirling slowly in a draught. As she climbed on to the bed, her foot kicked against the cupboard doors, which slid open a little. When she swung back down to look inside, she saw her panda blanket folded carefully, freshly washed and sweet-smelling. She must have fallen asleep without it last night. Somehow this seemed important, as though she had taken a big step forward through an invisible door into a new, more grown-up way of living. But it would always be her favourite and she would keep it close by, wherever she went.

She reached for the star and took it down, holding it in her hand, feeling the roughness of its edges.

The star had worked.

Emily paused at the top of the stairs and looked at the scene below. Dad was in his chair, smiling. Josie was perched on one of the arms, her cheeks flushed pink from the heat of the fire and the glass of wine in her hand. Nana Godwin sat on the sofa, so close below her that she could have jumped right into Nana's lap except Alexander was already curled up there, fast asleep.

It wasn't the same as any other Christmas she'd ever had.

But perhaps it was enough.

Slowly, she made her way down the stairs and across the room to the Christmas tree. She stretched up and hung the star right on the top. After all, she didn't need to hang it in the window anymore; everyone she wanted to be home for Christmas was here.

Well, not quite everyone. The Mum-shaped hollow inside her swelled and throbbed for a moment, like the pain in her hand. Perhaps it would never go away. But perhaps she didn't really want it to.

She stayed gazing at the star for a while to hide her tears. Nobody spoke; there was only the pop and crackle of the fire.

Dad broke the silence by clearing his throat. 'I brought this back from the farm last night.' He held out the dark-blue parcel Dibs had given her. 'You dropped it when you stood up. I hope it's nothing breakable. You'd better open it and check.'

Emily felt shy all of a sudden as everyone watched her dig her nails under the sticky tape and peel off the paper.

She gave a gasp. There, amid the wrapping, was her clock! The alarm clock that she had left in the outhouse. Dibs knew – had known all along – that she was the one who had taken Lotta and hidden her. Even though he hated having the lynx around, he hadn't betrayed her. What a good friend he had been, after all.

'That's a strange sort of present,' said Dad. 'It looks very like your old one. Why has he given you that?'

Emily opened and closed her mouth, trying to think of something to say.

Josie came to her rescue. 'Maybe he thought it was something you needed.'

Nana held out her arm for a hug and Emily burrowed in beside her on the sofa. She stroked

Alexander's soft head and chin, feeling the vibration of his purr.

'Maybe he did,' she said. 'Who knows what he was thinking?' She caught Josie's eye and winked. 'We all have our secrets, don't we?'

Acknowledgements

To all my writing friends who have supported me through thick and thin. I would never have got this far without you, so this book is a joint effort really! Special thanks to Andy Smart for your incisive eye, as well as Andrea, Alan, Marie-Claire, Jenny, Jackie, Natalia and Bazz, SCBWI friends and all the Book Frizzers. To my agent, Lucy Juckes, for believing in me and my writing, and the wonderful Firefly team for launching this book into the world. Thank you all.

Firefly

At Firefly we care very much about the environment and our responsibility to it. Many of our stories involve the natural world, our place in it and what we can all do to help it, and us, survive the challenges of the climate emergency.

Go to our website **www.fireflypress.co.uk** to see some of our great environmental stories.

We are always looking at reducing our impact on the environment, including our carbon footprint and the materials we use, and are taking part in UK-wide publishing initiatives to improve this wherever we can.

Keeper of Secrets is fictional, but there are many charities and groups across the UK working to restore and protect our natural world. This may range from planting trees to creating marine protection areas to reintroducing birds and animals. As Sarah's book shows, these are complex problems, and different areas and animals need different solutions, but it is exciting to remember that we can all actively improve our environment.